I MARRIED THREE BOYS

ROYAL HAREM
BOOK FOUR

LEXIE MIERS

CHAPTER 1

ERIN

Lights, camera, action.

Viktor, Silas and I waited in the wings—well, one wing in particular of the royal suites in Lichstein's castle—as Henryk went through the motions of another pained performance for a member of the royal press. From the moment we stepped off the helicopter, they clamored for a place in line along the hall that led to a ballroom used for press conferences and interviews. It was exhausting, and I wasn't even the one under the glare of the spotlight. I knew what these interviews cost Henryk. The set of his shoulders and jaw, the firm line he'd mashed his lips into, every little crease at the corners of his eyes spoke volumes.

And at the front of the line, choreographing the parade of reporters, was the one and only Harlow.

Keep your friends close and your enemies closer. That old adage had most certainly been written about people like her. Power hungry, ruthless and with zero sense of remorse, the woman was known for writing stories without thought or care for any of the ramifications for the parties involved, save herself and what salacious details could advance her career. Henryk said we should be grateful she was on our side.

She should be grateful I hadn't resorted to violence.

Viktor, Silas and I weren't convinced of her newfound loyalty to the crown. Skeptical was our middle names. The woman lacked a moral compass and would have sold out her source for the lead public relations position to the royal family if she actually had a name.

What would happen if someone came along with a better offer? She'd no doubt take it and run.

Still, the woman stepped into her newly appointed role and fulfilled her duties to Henryk and the crown with an ease I almost envied. If I wanted to be at Henryk's side in any capacity, I would have to learn to navigate the press and control the narrative.

Like she did.

Harlow was comfortable in front of the cameras and not afraid to take charge, putting more than one reporter and camera person in their place when they overstepped and went off the approved official talking points.

While I hadn't forgiven her for the stories she'd printed while working for the tabloids, she protected Henryk and the royal family from people like herself and for the time being, that was good enough for now.

"How's he holding up?" Viktor sidled up behind me, wrapped his arm around my waist and draped the other over my left shoulder, pulling me close.

His fingers brushed back and forth over my breast. The light friction between the thin silk of my blouse and lace bra, combined with the promise of things to come, tightened my nipples. Safe behind the thick velvet drapes that separated the entrance from the press room to the wing which held the private residences, Viktor was free to take liberties that Henryk was not.

At least, not until we were behind closed doors. Something I was very much looking forward to.

"He's exhausted. Look at him." I tilted my head back, glanced up at Viktor and watched him watching Henryk.

At some point, back on that deserted island, the tension between them evolved into something else. The emotion that simmered in

Viktor's eyes as he looked at Henryk filled my heart with joy. He tolerated Henryk at first, grew to like him the more time we spent together, and yet, I wasn't sure he would ever appreciate or care for him the way I did. But in that moment, any doubts I had were gone. Viktor saw the same qualities in Henryk that I did, and he loved him too.

Henryk wasn't just my prince. He was ours.

"Don't worry, babe." Viktor's right hand slipped into the pocket of my dress slacks, gripping my inner thigh while he massaged my breast with his left and nuzzled into my neck. "Silas is already drawing a bath and chilling the champagne. We know how to help Henryk relax better than anyone, right? We'll take good care of him."

I shifted in his arms, tracing my parted lips with the tip of my tongue until Viktor positioned himself to accept the invitation and claimed my mouth with his. He explored every inch of my mouth, devouring me, reminding me of all the other things he could do with just his tongue. I pulled back, knowing my lips were plump and a little pink from the passion he poured into the kiss.

"Yes, we will." My voice was husky with the need I felt in every fiber of my being.

We hadn't been together, the three of us alone in bed, since our rescue, and I ached to touch them, to feel the press of their bodies against mine—not just in the act but in the aftermath that followed. That blissful, lazy glow, a tangle of sheets and people sharing all of themselves. Which was something I planned to rectify just as soon as Henryk finished this interview.

Viktor was a contractor, which meany he was good with his hands, especially in the bedroom, and he sure as hell knew how to build anticipation. Heat pooled between my legs, and my body was thrumming with desire as he moved from light petting to something heavier. There was a chance—albeit a small one—the risk, the thrill heightened every touch.

Of course, I never would have risked it if I didn't think we were safe behind the curtain. The last thing any of us wanted to do was make things any more difficult for Henryk than they already were.

That was the whole point of our surprise—to help him relax. Another scandal was that last thing he needed. Which is precisely why Ray, the head of Henryk's personal security and the two royal guards, handpicked for their skills and discretion, stood between the press corps and the hall leading to the private living quarters of the castle.

Just as Viktor took me to the edge, heightening the anticipation and leaving me at a fever pitch, a reporter could be heard shouting his question over Harlow's announcement that the press conference was over.

"And what about the rumors, your highness?" The reporter's voice and the direction his question was headed felt like someone had poured a five-gallon bucket of ice-cold water on top of us.

Viktor stiffened, and not in the way he had a moment ago. His hands stilled before he pulled them away altogether and put a respectable distance between us, as if he expected someone to rip the heavy velvet curtain back, revealing our hiding spot.

"The prince has finished answering questions. Thank you for your time." It sounded like Harlow was trying to get ahead of any other outbursts and escort Henryk out of the room. "This way, Your Highness."

But the hasty exit was like chumming in shark infested waters—a huge mistake.

"People are talking, Prince Henryk. Your people." The reporter was relentless, shouting his questions over the murmurs of the rest of the press corps and Harlow's insistence that the interview was over. "Don't you want to assure your country that your engagement and upcoming nuptials aren't a well-orchestrated cover for your less conventional lifestyle?"

"That's enough. We're done here. Any additional questions for the prince or the royal family can, as always, be submitted to my office." Harlow's voice grew louder and the clack of her heels against the marble tiles louder as she approached, no doubt ushering Henryk toward the curtain and the privacy afforded behind it.

"Prince Henryk! Your highness!" the reporter called after him.

"This is your chance to convince Lichtenstein that you're not a fake. Don't you have something you want to say?"

Viktor And I stepped back, flattening ourselves against the wall and keeping out of sight as Henryk and Harlow yanked the curtain back and stormed into the hall.

"This press conference was a futile endeavor. We're supposed to be controlling the narrative." Henryk slapped his palm against the pristine white wall, leaning on it for support.

"I guess the story of a prince being rescued from a deserted island and safely returned to his homeland isn't playing as well as you hoped?" Viktor rested his hand on Henryk's shoulder and gave a gentle squeeze. "A new story will come along, some disaster or something and they'll move on, right?"

"Is that where we are? Hoping for a natural disaster to distract the press from the one unraveling in my life?" Henryk dipped his chin and shook his head, an exasperated sigh falling from his otherwise perfect, kissable lips.

"Is that what we are? A disaster that needs to be mitigated?" I tried to stifle my hurt feelings over his choice of words, but the sting was there, and I couldn't hide it.

The plan for a romantic afternoon, escaping the stress and worries of real life outside the castle in the warmth of each other's arms, was slipping away like grains of sand through fingers. All our preparations, the surprises Silas was even now putting the finishing touches on, were wasted.

The frustration in Henryk's eyes when his head snapped up and he met my gaze was proof enough he'd heard it. "That's not what I meant."

"But it's what you said." I slipped my hand into Viktor's, lacing our fingers together, and led him back to the guest suite we shared with Silas, leaving our prince and the hopes for a romantic afternoon behind.

The battle for what Henryk wanted and what was expected of him had never been more evident, and I was terrified now that he was back in the castle he was losing the fight.

That we were going to lose him.

CHAPTER 2

HENRYK

I had my reservations about bringing Harlow into the fold. Giving someone who previously had no qualms about splashing my private life all over the tabloids access to the inner circle of the royal family and Erin, Viktor and Silas, took a huge leap of faith and a hell of a lot of desperation. But she proved herself by intercepting the throng of reporters waiting at the royal gates like an opposing army before the helicopter even touched down on the helipad after our rescue. And again today, shutting down the press conference and ushering me out of the room before things got out of hand.

If only she could have silenced that one reporter. If only I had taken better care to choose my words before complaining about it. The rest of my day, my time spent with Erin, Viktor and Silas, would have gone differently. Instead, I let the mounting pressures upon my return get to me and unintentionally suggested that our relationship was a disaster when that couldn't have been further from the truth.

A man could consider himself lucky to find love with one person, but three? I wouldn't have thought it possible hadn't Erin, Viktor and Silas walked back into my life. My time with them was the one silver lining to the arranged marriage with Posy. If not for my mother's insistence that I take a bride—one of her choosing, of course—the royal advisors would never have uncovered the vows four children shared in the middle of a playground before they were old enough to understand the ramifications of the promises they'd made to each other. If not for the arranged marriage, I never would have seen them again.

That and the memories we made over the last few weeks would be enough to see me through my duties to the crown and country. Unless, of course, I figured a way out of the marriage. Which should have been my top priority, and it would be if not for the relentlessness of the press corp. I wasted more time in front of the cameras rehashing the events of my attempted kidnapping and the days spent on the island while waiting to be rescued at the same time tiptoeing around the topic of Erin, Viktor and Silas, when I should have been breathing down the neck of my advisor to find a loophole in the marriage contract my mother had arranged on my behalf.

The suite was quiet, with no sign of Erin, Viktor or Silas in the main sitting area that adjoined the bedrooms with ensuite baths to an unused kitchen, thanks to the culinary staff available to castle residents, day or night. They wouldn't have roamed far from the guest wing. They weren't looking to make headlines again any more than I was. If we learned one thing in Ibiza, it was that private was not the same thing as privacy.

My petulant brother and his spy drones made sure of that.

An open bottle of champagne bobbed in a bucket of ice water, beads trailing down the outside to pool on the silver tray beneath it, taunting me from across the room. The three empty glasses beside it as a stark reminder of what we could have been doing if I hadn't acted like a jerk.

Rather than let a perfectly good Dom go to waste, I snatched the bottle from the ice bucket, leaving a trail of water droplets on the rug on my way to the couch. Sprawled across the cushions, a leg draped over the side, I drowned my self-pity in expensive champagne. I could almost feel my mother's disappointment, see the frown settled onto her typically stoic face. Knowing that she was as unhappy with my recent behavior as I was, with the future she'd planned for me felt like cause to celebrate and there was more than enough bubbly to get the job done.

Though I would much rather have been sharing it with Erin, Viktor and Silas.

Murmured voices from the furthest bedroom broke the silence and the morose thoughts invading my mind. They were still here, in the suite. A part of me feared they had packed their things and left. A bigger part of me felt they would have been right to do so. Now that we were back in Lichtenstein, it was getting very difficult to see any future that had them in it. At least one that they all deserved.

And yet my heart, the most important part of me, the one I kept hidden from the rest of the world, rejoiced in knowing they stayed despite the ruthlessness of the press and the rigidity of my family. I needed to quit sulking and try to salvage the rest of the afternoon. Champagne still in hand, I pushed off the couch, grabbed the tray with the crystal flutes and prepared myself to make a three-part apology.

I rapped the bottom of the bottle against the door and cleared my throat. "May I come in?"

"Henryk." Erin yanked open the door and grabbed a fistful of my shirt. The crystal champagne flutes clinked together, threatening to topple off the serving tray as she tugged me inside the bedroom. "How long have you been here? We didn't even hear you come in."

"I'm surprised you didn't. The thoughts racing inside my head were loud enough that I assumed everyone within the castle walls could hear them. Dom Perignon seemed like a good distraction."

Seeing the three of them together, lounging around in the bedroom, stirred up more than just memories of the days and nights we'd spent together.

"Of course, there are other, more enjoyable ways to distract oneself." I wanted that, for us to be in bed together. To see Erin's golden locks splayed across the satin sheets, those sapphire eyes wild with passion, ecstasy poised on those perfect, pouty lips as we ravished her.

But first, I needed to remove my foot from my mouth and apologize for my rash words and for hurting her feelings.

"I'm sorry, Erin. And to you too, Viktor and Silas. Coming home… being here is harder than I thought it would be and I'm not myself. Or at least I don't feel like myself. Not the man who left this castle a few weeks ago and certainly not the version of myself that I want to be and feel like I actually can be when I'm with the three of you. I don't think this—what we share—is a disaster. Far from it. Our reunion has been the best thing to happen to me since the day we made promises to each other all those years ago."

"Oh, Henryk, if anyone should be apologizing, it's me."

Erin took the tray of glasses from my hand and passed them to Viktor, who'd already gotten off the bed to do the same.

"It wasn't fair for me to put words in your mouth. I know that's not what you meant. This is…it's a lot…I mean we're all stressed." She waved her hand, gesturing to all three of them. "I can only imagine how much stress you're feeling, and I really wasn't trying to add to that."

"You're not. None of this is your fault, any of you. If my brother hadn't—"

"Hush." Erin stepped forward, closing the last few inches that separated us and pressed her finger to my lips, rendering me speechless with that one touch. "We finally have you to ourselves and I, for one, don't want to waste a second of our time together talking about your brother or the crown or stupid reporters."

"Neither do I." I spared a glance over her shoulder at Viktor and Silas, who both smiled and nodded their approval while they lounged in the bed as if anticipating where Erin and I would end up.

My hands found their way to her hips, pulling her tightly against my body before working their way around to grab her ass. She tilted her head back, giving me access to nip and kiss the length of her neck. We worked the buttons of each other's shirts, stripping layers of clothes as I backed her toward the bed to Viktor and Silas, who were eagerly removing their own clothing and tossing them to the floor.

We fell on the bed, tangled together and into the waiting arms of the two other men who completed our quartet.

Viktor positioned Erin in the center of the mattress, lying beside on her left, while Silas took the space on her right, leaving me front and center. They each hooked an arm under her knees and lifted her legs, spreading her wide open. She let out a soft moan, arching her back as they simultaneously laved at her breasts, circling her taut nipples with their tongues before pulling them into their mouths. She was hot, wet and fucking glorious. It was all the invitation I needed. I buried my face between her legs, licking, sucking and nipping at her clit until she teetered on a cliff of ecstasy.

"Come for me, Erin. I want to feel and taste you come." I slipped two fingers inside her, easing them in and out, teasing until I felt that first pulsing throb, then picked up the pace, pushing her over the edge into orgasm.

After that, we took our time exploring each other, exploring Erin. She gave as much, if not more than she took, making sure that we all shared in the ecstasy. She was the true princess of my heart. A goddess, Aphrodite reincarnated, and I wanted nothing more than to spend the rest of my life worshiping at the temple that was her body. The way Viktor and Silas lazily stroked her as we basked in that blissful state after lovemaking where our most basic, carnal needs were satisfied and nothing existed beyond our bed, I knew they felt the same way.

The afternoon slipped into evening, and I was forced to tear myself away and fulfill yet another obligation. Not to the crown, but to my mother. And this time I wasn't the only one. The queen had invited everyone to dinner.

We showered—which would have gone faster had that been done individually, but every second spent under the hot spray of water together was worth making my mother wait—and dressed in the appropriate eveningwear that I had procured for everyone and joined the royal family in the formal dining hall.

Posy was seated to my mother's right, and an empty chair for me sat across from her on my mother's left. My brother, Nicky, raised a glass and smirked in response to my grimace over the seating arrangement. He seemed to delight in anything that caused me discomfort.

Jealousy was a wicked temptress and my brother had long been under its seduction.

I took my seat opposite my arranged fiancée and as far from my three lovers as the dining table would allow.

The queen clacked a silver fork against the crystal goblet in front of her and raised the glass in toast. "To the happy couple."

Everyone raised their glass and sipped their wine, but none shared in the queen's enthusiasm. Which didn't bother her in the slightest. The queen got what the queen wanted. In this case, a marriage for the heir to the woman she deemed a suitable royal match.

"I am sure all will be delighted to know that I have completed the arrangements, and the ceremony will commence in two weeks." My mother sipped her wine before returning the goblet to its precise spot in the place setting and sipped her spoon into the first course—a bowl of soup.

Posy choked on the broth and reached for the napkin in her lap, dabbing the corners of her mouth to cover her cough. "Two weeks, Your Grace?"

The queen's curt nod was her final word and brooked no argument. My fate was sealed. In fourteen days, I gained a wife and lost everything I'd ever loved.

CHAPTER 3

VIKTOR

I'd had more fun at funerals than dinner with the royal family. Henryk's mother, the queen, was a real piece of work. And his father wasn't much better. He just sat there without a care, and never said a word as his wife ruined their son's life. It was obvious what Henryk wanted, and it wasn't the woman seated across from him at the dining table.

And to think I actually envied him.

Shit, my family was a mess. I learned more about my family history from knowing about their rap sheets than from time spent with anyone actually related to me. I was in and out of foster homes, dreaming of what life would be like if I had a real family to take care of me. To love me.

But if this was what motherly love looked like, I was glad I'd missed out.

The main course hadn't arrived, and I was already feeling sorrier for our prince than I had in all the days we spent together. He was miserable. And it didn't escape my attention that his fiancée wasn't thrilled with the queen's announcement either. She was up to something, and I needed to find out what.

We had enough problems with the spare heir.

The last thing we needed was Henryk's so-called fiancée making trouble. Posy made it clear that not only was she not in love with the prince, but he wasn't her type. In every way possible. Princess Posy already had a girlfriend, and she had every intention of keeping her. But she was also loyal to both her throne and Henryk's and was willing to do whatever necessary to ensure the success of both their countries. And that included keeping her preferences and her love interest hidden from the public eye. Apparently, the girlfriend agreed, because I didn't see anyone else throwing a pity party in the castle's guest wing besides the four of us.

Still, my gut was telling me Posy was working an angle, making moves behind the scenes that weren't about her wedding to Henryk - or at least not entirely. My gut was almost always right. Admittedly, I was a little out of my element in a foreign country. Jet lag, time zones, different food and all that shit. But when it came down to it, I trusted my instincts. Which meant confronting Posy.

Of course, getting a princess alone was easier said than done. Enlisting Ray's help was probably my best bet there.

I'd talk to him after dessert or whatever course that ended royal dinners. I lost track after the third plate and sherbet palate cleanser. Still, the royal chefs and their staff outdid themselves. It blew my mind that people ate food like this every night. If it didn't come from a drive-thru, the only hot dinners I had came out of a microwave. Long days on the construction site often ran into longer nights in the office, taking care of the business side of things with Silas. Cooking wasn't going to happen. It was a damn good thing I had a physically demanding job, or all that fast food might catch up to me.

The multicourse meal may have ended with Créme Brulé but our night with the royal family was far from over. Brandy was being served in the billiard room. A billiard room. I shook my head, stifling a laugh as we made our way to the massive room with rich wood paneling, intricately carved wood trim highlighted with gold leaf, crystal chandeliers, a wall of floor-to-ceiling windows that over-looked the gardens, a full bar and the finest leather furniture. It was a far cry from the pool hall Silas, and I frequented on Friday nights back home, that's for damn sure.

But it gave me an opportunity to talk to Ray, who was leaning against the bar nursing a club soda.

"Any news on our friend?" I asked, reaching for the decanter of what I hoped was whiskey.

"The drone footage was traced back to the servers here at the castle, but that isn't enough to convince the queen. Any one of the staff members could access the internet. As for the secure servers? Outside my team and the royal family, there's only a handful of employees who have authorization, but that's still not enough to convince her of precious little Nicky's involvement in the public humiliation of her first born. The king, maybe. But I want something irrefutable."

Ray plucked the wedge of lime from the rim of his glass, squeezed the juice into the soda and dunked the fruit beneath the ice cubes. He took a sip and placed the drink on a coaster, absently spinning the glass around on the highly polished countertop as he spoke.

"Harlow is working her way through the email trail. If we can prove Nicky or one of his staff sent the videos to the press, then we've got something. He could still argue his accounts were hacked, but the king and queen will be more likely to believe Henryk's side of the story."

"It's not a story." I slammed the amber liquid, relishing the burn as it traveled to my stomach. "Nicky is sabotaging his brother and the royal family along with it. He's putting a negative spin on everything to make Henryk look bad. To make Erin look bad."

"But not you or Silas?" Ray glanced at his watch before reaching for a decanter of clear alcohol and adding a shot to his cup. "Officially off the clock."

He nodded and lifted his glass toward the two guards who, like clockwork, entered the game room and stood off to the side of a professional card table that could have graced the floor at the most expensive casino in Vegas.

"So, about you and Silas... you're not worried about your reputations?" Ray prodded and pulled a cigar from the inside pocket of his suit jacket and motioned toward the door that led out to the veranda. "Cuban, my one vice. Though I rarely allow myself the indulgence anymore."

"As far as vices go, there's probably worse ones." I clasped a hand on his shoulder, enjoying the camaraderie with the off-duty version of Ray, and followed him outside to continue our conversation. "Silas and I own our own business, and bad press is bad for business, that's true enough. But our business is also construction and well, this type of scandal isn't going to do irreparable damage to us like it could Erin. She's not her own boss and has to get past the gatekeepers if she wants to get ahead."

"You don't think a call from the royal family would grant her that access?" Ray pulled a small cigar cutter from his pocket and snipped the head of the cigar over the railing and toasted the end over the flame of his lighter. "Because Henryk would do anything and everything in his power to make things easier for the three of you back home."

"This isn't about what we can get from the crown, Ray. I told you, Silas and I make our own way, and Erin will too when this all blows over. Which it will. Sooner back in the States than in Europe, because we have plenty of celebrities doing stupid shit every day," I groused, crossing my arms over my chest. "Nicky needs to be taught a lesson in morality."

"So, this is about payback?" The orange glow illuminated Ray's dark eyes as he took a drag from the cigar, blowing smoke rings on the exhalation. The sweet and spicy scent of the burning tobacco hung in the air between us.

"Maybe. Do you have a problem with that?" I watched his train of smoke rings expanding as they drifted off until they dissipated altogether.

"Not at all." Ray held the cigar between his teeth and smiled. "I was just making sure your priorities were in order."

Oh, my priorities were definitely in order. Ray didn't have to worry about that. I'd dealt with my fair share of spoiled, entitled assholes like Nicky, and they all had the same thing in common. They can dish it, but they can't take it. He was the black sheep of the royal family, not Henryk, and I was more than happy to give the king and queen a little reminder about what their second son was really like.

Because it sure as shit wasn't the doting, well behaved son that toed the family line he'd been pretending to be since news broke about Henryk's relationship with Erin, Silas and me.

"How well do you know the princess?" I already had one poker in the fire with Nicky and was about to add another one with Henryk's fiancée.

"Posy?" Ray stubbed out his cigar on the heel of his shoe, giving it one last longing look before tossing it in a wastebasket hidden in the patio's stonework. "She is as smart as she is stunning. A loyal ally or formidable adversary."

"I think she's up to something." I may have been overplaying my hand with Ray. He was loyal to Henryk, but the crown signed his checks.

"Oh, she's most certainly up to something." Ray laughed and clasped his hand on my forearm. "I believe she already told you she doesn't want this marriage any more than Henryk does."

"Good. So she's an ally then." I couldn't help the mischievous grin that settled on my face. "Do you think you could get me a meeting with her?"

"Oh, I think that could be arranged." Ray was fast becoming my co-conspirator and donned a smile that matched my own.

Things were falling into place, and with any luck, I would get the evidence Henryk needed to buy his freedom assuming he still wanted that. I had a few nagging doubts. With Henryk home and under his mother's thumb, he was falling back into the old routine of being the self-sacrificing heir to Lichtenstein. Still, I'd do whatever I could to give him the choice he never thought he had.

After that, it was up to him to decide.

CHAPTER 4

ERIN

Dinner with Henryk's family didn't go as well as I'd hoped. Not that I was expecting the feast to be held in our honor or anything, but I thought Viktor, Silas and I might have a chance to at least plead Henryk's case for not marrying Posy and for us to remain in his life—his public life.

Because a secret love affair was out of the question.

Regardless if Viktor and Silas agreed, though I was pretty sure they felt the same way I did, I couldn't and wouldn't live that way. There had been times in my life where I'd questioned whether or not I was good enough. Job interviews before landing the right marketing firm, pitches at work before landing the big client, and more than one night spent with an ex-boyfriend. But not one of those moments were with Viktor, Silas and Henryk.

Every minute we were together felt right. I never doubted myself, us, or the way we made each other feel. And I wouldn't ruin what we had by acting like it was something to be ashamed of and keeping it hidden. I didn't crave the limelight or celebrity status by being paraded around on the prince's arm, but I certainly didn't want to be stuck in the shadows like a dirty little secret.

The rest of the night didn't go according to plan either. The queen burst every bubble in our soaker tub with her announcement that the arrangements for the wedding had not only been made, but that the ceremony was two weeks away. None of us were feeling the least bit romantic after that.

Viktor, Silas and Henryk opted for eliminating the enemy on the newest map in their favorite PlayStation game, while I found solace in an oversized hot fudge sundae with extra fudge, whipped cream, rainbow sprinkles and a brownie on the side prepared by a world-class chef and streaming a late eighties dark comedy titled Throw Mama From the Train.

I stumbled out of my bedroom rubbing my temples and cursing the sunlight beaming through the large windows in search of coffee. This was my first and last sugar hangover. Coffee service had been provided along with an array of breakfast sweets that made my stomach roil and my head throb.

"Too soon. I don't care how delicious you look, cinnamon rolls, you're off the menu until further notice," I grumbled, more to myself than the three men still passed out on the couch with game controllers in hand, and swiped a mini quiche from the savories included in the breakfast spread.

A knock sounded at the door, and assuming it was a member of the royal staff coming to collect the coffee cart or clean the guest suite, I stuffed another bite sized quiche in my mouth and opened the door.

"Good morning, Erin." Posy, perky and perfect in a bright red designer dress that accentuated her model-like figure, with matching shoes and clutch purse tucked under her arm, stood in the hall. She peered into the suite, seeming to find what she was looking for when her gaze landed on Henryk with his legs propped up on the antique coffee table. "May I come in?"

Rather than wait for an answer, she strolled in like she owned the place. And in a way, I suppose she did. As Henryk's fiancée, she had more claim to this or any part of the castle than I did.

"Posy." I blew the steam off the surface of my coffee and took a sip, relying on the rich, nutty flavor of the dark roast and its caffeine content to ease my headache and give me the courage I needed to hear whatever it was the princess had to say.

Our interactions had been brief, and while she made it clear she didn't want to marry Henryk any more than he wanted to marry her, she was also prepared to sacrifice her own happiness and that of her girlfriend to fulfill their royal obligations.

And yet, Posy was the reason we were still in Lichtenstein and staying in the castle. If she hadn't invited us to take part in the wedding, we would have been on the first plane back to the States. It was obvious that a wedding to Henryk wasn't the only thing Posy had been planning.

Which is probably why the queen had taken matters into her own hands.

"I thought I would find him here." Her heels clacked against the floor as she strode across the suite to the couch where her fiancé—and my lover—was fast asleep. She poked him on the shoulder. "Wake up, Henryk. We have much to discuss and very little time, thanks to your mother."

"Can I get you some coffee?" I asked, brushing the specks of flaky quiche crust from my shirt. "Maybe a cinnamon roll or two...or ten?"

I might dislike Posy a little less if she put on a few pounds. Not that I was out of shape. I was the perfect weight for my height and loved my curves, but something about Posy's lithe frame and the way she walked on those pencil-thin heels made me self-conscious.

"Boys!" Posy clapped her hands together three times. "I'm supposed to be at a fitting in an hour, and that's not a lot of time for us to plan a coup."

"You want to overthrow the king and queen? I think you're looking for the wrong brother." Silas raised his arms over his head, arched his back and stretched, fighting through a yawn. "And I definitely need coffee before we talk about toppling governments."

He nudged Henryk and Viktor with his elbows before pushing off the couch and relieving me of the carafe of coffee. After filling four mugs, he passed them around, grabbed a muffin from a wicker basket on the serving cart and reclaimed the middle couch cushion.

"Thank you, Silas." Posy glanced at the cup, a small frown settling on her face at the lack of cream or sugar, returned it to its saucer and placed them both on the table. "Ray called this morning to request a meeting. Imagine my surprise to hear that it was at the bequest of Viktor, and not my fiancé."

The princess had a hell of a poker face. Her expression gave nothing away, but there was the slightest hint of amusement in her voice. Posy pointed to the empty chair to the left of the couch. "May I?"

"Oh, yeah. Sorry." Viktor raised his legs off the table and planted his feet on the floor to make a space for Posy to pass. "Thanks for coming by on such short notice."

"It took some work on my personal assistant's part, but she managed to rearrange my schedule." Posy lowered herself into the chair and smoothed the fabric of her dress over her knees. "But, as I said, I don't have a lot of time. The designer is notoriously bad-tempered, and I am not going to pricked and poked with sewing pins because I was late for my fitting."

"You really want to make that appointment? Because I was under the impression you didn't want to get married." Viktor took a sip of coffee, eyeing the princess over the rim of his cup. "At least not to Henryk."

"And I don't." She nodded toward Henryk, a smile playing at her glossy garnet-tinted lips. "No offense, darling. You know you're not my type. You lack certain physical attributes. Just because I don't want to marry Henryk, doesn't mean I'm not planning on getting married. If we work together, the wedding I want and the wedding I know the three of you want can be a reality."

"Whoa, hold up a sec. We don't want Henryk to marry you, but we rushed into a wedding once that ended with an annulment. There's a lot more involved this time around." Silas said what I assumed everyone was thinking.

Because it was definitely what I ran through my mind when Posy brought up a wedding for the four of us.

I wanted Henryk, Viktor and Silas and had no intention of sharing them with anyone, but marriage? Three of us were living our lives in a completely different country. We had families, friends, and careers. The logistics were overwhelming, and not something I wanted to think about at the moment.

"How about we take this one ceremony at a time?" My stomach roiled. Too much caffeine on an empty stomach. I swapped out my coffee for bottled water and grabbed a banana from the fruit basket, which I quickly switched out for an apple when three sets of eyes peered in my direction. Clearly, some of us were still juveniles when it came to produce.

"As long as Henryk and I aren't standing at the altar together two weeks from now, that's fine with me." Posy glanced at her watch, noting the time and how little we had left to formulate a plan.

"Ray, Harlow and I have been working on tying the photos and videos that were leaked to the paparazzi back to Nicky. Maybe they've got something we can use." Viktor fished his phone out of his pocket and scrolled through his messages, shaking his head. "Nothing yet."

"Proving Nicky is behind the tabloid stories will go a long way to smooth the king and queen's ruffled feathers where Henryk is concerned." Posy fidgeted with the diamond bracelet dangling around her wrist. "But I fail to see how that will stop Henryk and me from taking our vows."

"You could always refuse." I tossed the apple core in the wastebasket, grabbed a linen napkin from a stack on the cart and wiped my hands. "I mean, after all the headlines about orgies and affairs, the scandal alone would be enough for you to call off the wedding, right?"

"I suppose." Posy pursed her lips, seeming to mull over the idea of publicly breaking things off with Henryk. "Perhaps that should be a last resort. I'd rather not humiliate Henryk and embarrass either of our families unless I absolutely must."

"Yeah, the press would lap that up too. More scandalous headlines." Viktor raked his fingers through his hair, combing out his bedhead. "I'm with Posy on this one. Definitely a last resort."

"There are five of us and we have fourteen days." Posy stood, tucked her clutch back under her arm and headed for the door. "I'm sure we can come up with a suitable plan before then."

I wished I felt as confident as Posy sounded. I was fresh out of ideas, and one look at Viktor, Silas and Henryk told me they were too. In fourteen days, Henryk and Posy would commit themselves to one another.

For better or worse.

CHAPTER 5

SILAS

Two weeks. Fourteen days. Three hundred and thirty-six hours until everything went back to life before Liechtenstein. But who the hell was counting, anyway? Certainly, not me. Yeah, right. As if any of us could go back to the way things were. This wasn't the first time I shared a bed with more than one person. Or Viktor's. But it was the first time either of us considered making it permanent.

Why did Henryk have to be royalty?

I'm sure there were women—and men—all over the world who would love to land a prince, but our champagne wishes and caviar dreams were starting to feel more like a nightmare. Things would have been a hell of a lot easier if he worked construction like Viktor and me. The thought of Henryk on one of our job sites with a toolbelt strapped around his waist and a bright yellow hard hat on his head almost made me laugh. Almost. I was in a shitty mood, and I didn't see it ending any time soon.

Not unless we could find a loophole for Henryk to get out of a wedding that nobody seemed to want, except for the king and queen.

The fact that arranged marriages were still a thing blew my mind. Liechtenstein had medieval roots, but I didn't know they were still stuck in the dark ages. My mother set me up on a couple of blind dates with some of her friends' daughters, but negotiating a wedding contract? Hell no. She left my love life alone and quit her matchmaking ways when none of her attempts at finding a girlfriend made it past a first date. At the end of the day, the only thing my mom wanted was for me to be happy.

The same could not be said about the queen.

Granted, we didn't have a castle, a country, or any of the responsibilities that went along with it. Still, nothing ever came before her kids, and nothing ever would. The more time I spent around Henryk's family, the more grateful I was for mine. I wouldn't trade my parents for all the crown jewels in the king's vault.

Henryk was living proof that money didn't buy happiness. If it could, he would have bought his freedom a long time ago.

And now Posy expected us to come up with a plan to save them both. As much as I want a happy ending for all of us, I just wasn't sure that was possible anymore. I mean, if a future king and queen couldn't find a loophole in their own laws, how the hell were two contractors and a marketing rep supposed to do it?

Erin came in from the balcony, a momentary distraction from the negative thoughts running on a loop inside my head. But the sway of her hips as she walked toward me was just another painful reminder that there might not be a happily ever after at the end of this fairytale. She plopped down on the couch, the soft cushions swallowing her up as she grabbed a throw pillow, clutching it to her chest. She burrowed her face against it, but not before I saw the glassy sheen and reddish tint in her eyes.

Shit. She'd been crying again.

She tried to hide her tears from us, not wanting to make the situation any harder than it already is for Henryk, but the puffiness and blotchy skin were a dead giveaway. Even miserable, she was still the most beautiful woman I'd ever seen and I couldn't imagine my life without her.

But unless we all came up with a plan to stop the wedding, I'm going to have to.

"I've heard misery loves company." I said, aiming for a joke but hitting too close to the truth. I knew how much the idea of losing Henryk was tearing her up because I felt it too.

"Then it's a good thing you came to sit next to me." She lowered the pillow, sniffling as she mustered up a half smile and curled up against my side. "What are we going to do, Silas? It can't end like this. We can't let them get married."

"We're not." Viktor strolled out from our bedroom and joined us on the couch. "We're going to come up with something. We have to, because Henryk belongs with us."

"I know he does." She sniffled, fighting back fresh tears, and readjusted her position until she was sandwiched between the both of us, one side pressed against each of us. "And I know he wants that too."

"What if we can't? I mean, the king and queen have had a lifetime to arrange this wedding, and we've only got two weeks to crash it. That's not a lot of time." I shook my head at Viktor, and pressed my finger to Erin's lips, stifling any protests before they had a chance to make them. "Just hear me out, okay? What if the only way we can keep Henryk is staying here, in secret?"

"A dirty secret." Erin fisted her hands and rubbed them against her eyes, choking back another sob.

"It doesn't have to be, at least not to us. We know how much he cares about you... about all of us." I rested my hand on her leg, my fingers tracing lazy circles on her thigh. "So, I'll ask you again. If that's the only way we can have him, would you do it?"

Part of me hoped she'll say no.

I didn't want to hide our relationship any more than she did. We shouldn't have to because some people didn't think it was normal. I mean, define normal. I don't have to live my life to anyone else's standards but my own. Besides, a union between the four of us would be recognized in Liechtenstein. It was fucking legal in Henryk's country, so, why did he have to live to a different standard? If it was good enough for the citizens, it should be good enough for the prince.

But the other part? Hell, the other part hoped she said yes. Because I didn't want this to end. I'd be a liar if I said that I wasn't worried

Erin would have second thoughts about our relationship if Henryk wasn't in it. Would she bail on Viktor and me? As much as I wanted to know the answer, I was terrified to find out. Just thinking about it was killing me.

Erin stole my heart when we were kids, and she never gave it back. After spending the last few weeks with her, I knew she was the reason none of my relationships worked—because none of them were Erin. I had been looking for her all these years and now that I'd found her, I didn't want to lose her again.

"No. Yes. I don't know." She rested her right hand on mine, lacing our fingers together and reached for Viktor with her left, entwining theirs the same way. "I'm not sure that I could give up my life, my independence, to just be kept in the shadows. I have family, friends, and I'm building a career. I mean, I could walk away from that if I knew we were going to start a real life together, but if you're asking me to throw away the life I've made for myself to live a lie? I don't think I can. Would either of you?"

"We spent years busting our asses making other people's dreams come true and only just started working on our own. I mean, our construction company is finally taking off." Viktor leaned forward and glanced at me and I gave him the confirmation that I knew he was searching for. "So, no. No matter how much we want this, for all of us to stay together, we wouldn't walk away from that to live a lie either."

"And I wouldn't ask you to." Henryk stepped inside the suite, closing the door behind him and leaning against it for support. The press schedule, constant meetings with event planners and the mounting pressures from his parents were wearing on the prince. He was exhausted and it was starting to show. Not a good look for His Royal Highness. "You shouldn't have to give anything up to be with me. Even if it's what you wanted, I couldn't allow it. I don't want that kind of life for any of you."

"And what do you want, Henryk?" Erin shifted, turning over onto her knees, arms resting on the back of the couch as she watched her prince. Our prince.

"I want this. To come home to this every single day of my life."

Henryk slipped off his custom Italian leather loafers and placed them near the door before stopping at the built-in bar and pouring himself a drink.

The ice clinked against the glass, breaking the brief moment of silence as the conversation stopped and we watched the prince slam the scotch and pour himself another.

"Show me what you want, Henryk." Erin was off the couch and unbuttoning her shirt before I knew what was happening. The pale lavender button down that she stole from Viktor's closet was on the floor, and her lace bra was the next thing to go. She unbuttoned her pants, shimmied them down her hips, then stepped out of them and stood there in nothing more than a tiny lace thong. "Show me how much you want us to stay here with you."

Fuck me. We'd better figure this out because Henryk wasn't the only one who wanted to come home to this every day.

CHAPTER 6

HENRYK

*L*ast night was incredible. I was still riding the afterglow of having Erin in my arms, experiencing the give and take of pleasure between the four of us. Viktor, Silas and I were there for her, fulfilling every desire, bringing every fantasy to life and somehow, she managed to do the same for each of us. She is the most giving, the most beautiful creature on the planet, inside and out. She is ours and we are hers unconditionally.

How was I supposed to walk away from this in thirteen days?

There could be worse people to be trapped with in an arranged marriage than Posy. Neither of us were buying into the bullshit that love came over time. She didn't want to marry me any more than I wanted to marry her, but we do care for each other in the framework of a lifelong friendship built on mutual respect for each other's devotion to their country. There would be no expectations to maintain a happy marriage beyond the public eye, to force the other to try to make a life where there was none.

I would welcome her girlfriend into the palace under the guise of the princess's personal assistant if that was what she wished, and according to Posy, she does. She'd rather live with Posy in secret than without. And actually, they could live together with no one the wiser. An affair with one person is far easier to coordinate and cover up than an affair with three.

Damn. Was I really so weak that I would even consider asking them to stay? To give up their lives to be with me out of the public eye, behind closed doors? To live a lie?

After last night, I knew the answer was a resounding yes.

Watching them walk away would break me, leaving me a shell of the man I used to be. My heart and soul would shatter into a million pieces. Irreparable damage. Erin, Viktor and Silas had done the impossible. They saw right through my veneer, peeled off my carefully constructed mask, exposing the real man beneath. In just a few short weeks they leveled me. I would crawl on hands and knees without an ounce of shame and beg them to stay, to let me keep them.

Keep them? What was wrong with me? I loved them so much that I thought I might actually be losing my mind. They weren't something to possess. I couldn't just keep them.

But the clock was ticking, and I need to make a decision. Follow my heart or fulfill my duty? It was the twenty-first goddamn century and I shouldn't have to do either, but the royal family stood on tradition. Time marched slowly for royalty. Unless, of course, the queen was planning your wedding.

And then it felt like a military parade marching right over your heart.

As if on cue, my mother called and demanded my presence in her office to discuss yet another wedding detail. She knew I didn't care about whatever the chef was planning, how many layers the cake would have, what kind of flowers would decorate the venue, or which of the historic cathedrals favored by the royals for centuries would ultimately be chosen for the ceremony. None of it mattered.

I couldn't refuse her. I never had. But on this? Perhaps I should.

"Henryk." My mother, my queen, rose from the velvet-lined oak chair behind her desk, clasping her hands together. "Thank you for joining me for tea. There are things we need to discuss."

"What arrangements need my approval now, Mother?" The thought of sitting through another discussion over the minutiae of a royal wedding just added to my sour mood.

"Have a seat, my son." She gestured toward the arrangement of seventeenth century sofas with matching chairs and the serving tray laden with tea and assortment of sweet and savory pastries. With a snap of her fingers, she addressed the remaining staff in her office. "Leave us."

"Honestly, Mother." I didn't even bother to hide the disdain or roll of my eyes over the way she barked at her staff. It had always been a point of contention between us. Unlike my mother, I am appreciative of the fact that fortune of birth were all that separated me from the citizens of Liechtenstein. "Is it so difficult for you to try a little kindness when interacting with your staff? The air of indifference is a tired cliche."

"And you could try a little less indifference when it comes to your future wife. A petulant prince is yet another tired cliche." She sat on the sofa beside me, dropping two cubes of sugar in each china cup before pouring the tea.

To some, it would be a great honor to be served by the queen. For me, it was just another meeting that I no longer wished to attend. It seemed my mother isn't the only indifferent royal in the room. Though we are behaving in such a way for two entirely different reasons.

"Petulant? Are we here to discuss Nicky, then? What has the little scoundrel gotten himself into now?" I had other, more fitting names for my brother but none befitting a queen—or a mother's ear. It was enough that I was choosing to aggravate her by bringing up Nicky when it was more than obvious she was talking about me.

"Henryk, enough." Her lips mashed into a pencil thin line as she set the cup on its saucer and placed them both back on the silver tray. "Do you believe that I have survived this long by your father's side as we rule a country by being naive?"

"Of course not, Mother." *Cold and calculating, perhaps. Naive? Never.*

"And do you think a country the size of Liechtenstein continues to flourish in an ever-changing global market because your father and I live selfish lives, putting our own desires before the needs of our citizens?"

"Mother, please." The delicate porcelain cup rattled on its saucer and tea sloshed over the rim as I set it down on the tray untouched. "I have heard this speech since I was a little boy. I am well aware of what is expected of me."

"Well, it is clear to your father and I that you are in need of a reminder," she snapped, her voice sharper than the king's favorite cutlass. "Your father has had his dalliances—"

"Just father?" I knew that she's had her share of dalliances as well.

If I didn't know better, I would have thought my brother was the result of one of them. We were such different people it, was difficult to believe we shared the same DNA.

"The point I am trying to make, Henryk, is that love is not a good enough reason to shirk your responsibilities to this family, to the crown, to the country." Her hands were back in her lap, clasped together tightly enough to turn her knuckles white. "Your father and I care for each other. HIs mistresses are of no consequence to me or the way we rule."

"You act as if my feelings are treasonous. Does my love make me disloyal? My relationship would be accepted, permissible under the laws of this country." I abandoned her on the sofa and stormed over to the fireplace, gripping the marble mantlepiece for support.

"Accepted? You think the people of Liechtenstein would accept not only a princess but two prince consorts?" She let out a bitter laugh. "Tell me I didn't raise such a fool."

"Do you think so little of your own people?" Afraid the hand-carved stone would crumble between my fingers, I let go of the mantle, my hands clenching at my side as I turned to face her.

"We are held to a higher standard." She was on her feet, her temper flaring to match mine, her face reddened with the anger bubbling up from within her. "We hold ourselves to a higher standard."

My challenging behavior had no doubt pulled the cork on decades of emotions bottled up within her. She was not used to anyone questioning her authority, especially not me. I have always done what was expected of me—what she expects of me —without question.

Until now.

"This will not stand, Henryk. I forbid it." She jutted out her chin and doused my hot-tempered gaze with a glacial glare of her own.

"You forbid it?" A rebellious streak I never knew I had rose up within me, and I knew if she continued to push me, to force my hand, I would do the exact opposite of what she wanted. In the most glorifying, horrific way. "You would deny your own son the chance to be happy?"

"To save you from yourself? Yes, Henryk. I would." Her voice and expression softened to one never seen outside the castle walls and rarely seen by me.

For a moment she looked at me the way a mother would a son with all the love she felt but hardly ever showed. And then it was gone. The stoic, ice queen returned to rule over every aspect of my life.

"Think of your heritage. Your future. This family's future, Henryk. Our lineage cannot, it must not be in question. Ever. The royal line must continue in its purest form. Something that cannot be accomplished with one hundred percent certainty in a relationship with... multiple partners. One woman with three husbands? What if Viktor or Silas were to sire the first born? A challenge for the throne should never come from within the same house."

"I think that portion of your speech would be better served to Nicky." I was on the defensive, my spine stiff, shoulders squared, and arms folded across my chest. My body posture was closing me off from her. It wasn't a stance I would have ever taken with her before now.

"A few weeks ago, I would have said the same thing. But while one of my sons seems to be losing his grip on reality, the other seems to finally be coming to his senses." She narrowed her gaze, pinning me with her stare and the underlying threat.

"There is more than one person being naive in this room if you think that will work on me. Nicky is no more prepared to run this country than I am to answer your threats. Good day, Mother."

Without uttering another word, I turned my back on my mother and marched out of her office, desperate for the comfort and solace that could only be found with Erin, Viktor and Silas.

CHAPTER 7

VIKTOR

Nicky was a grifter, plain and simple. He may have the king and queen fooled, but I know a con man when I see one. Spend enough time in any aspect of the real estate business and one was bound to cross your path. Hell, a hundred of them could cross your path in a week. A boardroom or a throne room, it didn't make a difference. They're all the same. And I know when someone is lying. I've got a nose for it. If you couldn't smell a lie, you couldn't tell a lie. So, yeah, my bullshit meter is pretty good. Probably because I used to be pretty proficient in lying back when I was a kid in the foster care system.

Lying was just part of surviving.

But for a guy like Nicky it was just part of the game. He was playing everyone, especially his parents. He didn't give a shit about Liechtenstein. It wasn't about what he could do for his people, but what his people could do for him. He was just after the power, the glory, the wealth. He'd do whatever he could, tell whatever lies he had to in order to make that happen. He'd hurt anyone who got in his way.

Even his own brother

Nicky made that abundantly clear back in Ibiza. He took one look at Silas, Erin, and me and decided we were expendable. Nothing

45

more than collateral damage. Our family, friends, careers, and our privacy mean nothing to him. Wearing the crown is all he cared about.

If I were the king, I'd sleep with one eye open. Maybe double up on security, or bring back those poor fools who tasted the king's food to see if it was poisoned. I wouldn't turn my back on that asshole for a second. He'd probably just drive a knife into it.

Henryk seemed to think that digging up dirt on Nicky was a waste of time. On that, we would have to agree to disagree, because I couldn't shake the feeling that Nicky was the key to convincing the king and queen that Henryk, whether he had one partner or three, was the better choice for future king. No one was going to convince me that scouring the Liechtenstein law books was going to save our asses. The legal system took forever. I ought to know. I'd aged out of it.

Still, the fact that the king and queen were willing to overlook Nicky's already checkered past and skip over their first born spoke volumes about how they felt about Henryk's current love life.

Ray and I needed to come up with something good and do it quickly. The clock was ticking. We were already down a day, and so far, we had nothing. Nothing new, anyway. There was plenty of dirt where the spare heir was concerned but nothing freshly tilled. We needed something salacious, something that would rock the royal family and make their royal high-and-mighty-nesses forget how much they hated the idea of Henryk in a poly relationship.

As if being happy and in love were a bad thing.

What the hell did they know anyway? Look at them on TV, smiling and waving for the camera at another charity function that the people who were supposed to be benefiting couldn't even attend. They wouldn't know happiness if it came up and kicked them right in the crown.

I hated this shit. It pissed me off that anyone was making Henryk or Erin question the way they felt about Silas and me, and it pissed me off even more that it was his parents doing it. Loving us didn't make him crazy or irresponsible or immoral. Poly relationships were legal here. Unless, of course, you were the future king. Then all bets were off.

It was just one boring-ass wife for the rest of your life.

Posy seemed like a nice woman, but Henryk didn't love her, and she definitely didn't love him. He was lacking some pretty significant qualities for the princess' tastes. Posy and her partner didn't deserve to be forced into this crap any more than we did, but neither of them would walk away from the royal obligation of the arranged marriage. The princess' girlfriend has already agreed to be her mistress. She'd rather be a secret than single, which was why Posy was helping us as much as she could. She didn't want that sort of life for her girlfriend any more than Henryk did for the three of us.

The suite was quiet. Everyone else had gone to bed, and I risked another glance at the clock. It was almost midnight. Another day had come and gone, and we had nothing to show for it. The numbers flickered and switched from eleven-fifty-nine to twelve o'clock.

Officially twelve hours left.

I needed a distraction. Some background noise. Something to at least slow the train of thoughts circling in my head so I could focus. I was too wrapped up in emotion when what I needed was some damn logic. I snatched the remote off the coffee table and started flipping through the channels for something routine to watch, like one of those home renovation shows. House flipping couples rehabbing dilapidated historic homes was a guilty pleasure and might drown out the noise inside my head so I could friggin' think.

But Nicky's face was taunting me from the television, smiling and waving for the camera like he was already the crowned prince. That smug son of a bitch. *Click.* I smashed the channel button on the remote again. Nicky, at an airbase in his honorary uniform. *Click.* Another channel, another clip of Nicky. This time at a children's hospital. *Click.* More fucking Nicky. Before I even realized it, the remote was out of my hand and smashing up against one of the throw pillows on the opposite couch. Good thing it wasn't the wall. I hated plaster repair work.

A podcast seemed like a safer bet for background noise. I dug my earbuds out of my pocket, popped them in my ears and grabbed my phone, scrolling through the options in my subscriptions, but instead of making a selection, I fired off a text to Harlow.

Maybe it was the image of Nicky in front of the children's hospital stuck in my head. Maybe it was my own fucked-up childhood, but I had an idea. I wasn't sure if Henryk would like it, but at least I had an idea.

Me: **We need to dig deeper. We've been looking into the last few months, but Nicky was already putting things in motion. He was going to make a move on Henryk at some point. We just presented an opportunity and an easy target.**

Harlow: **It's after midnight.**

Me: **Closer to one, actually.**

Harlow: **Being an ass before sunrise or coffee is not going to inspire my best investigative work.**

Me: **Please, you love this. It's the best of both worlds. Tabloid trash and upper crust society.**

Harlow: **The rich do have better scandals.**

Me: **They can afford to. Which is also how they hide them so well.**

Harlow: **Not from me, they don't.**

Me: **Have I mentioned how glad I am that you're on our side now?**

Harlow: **Henryk said the same thing. Anything in particular that you're looking for?**

Me: **I was thinking we should take a look at old girlfriends, starting with ones that have a kid.**

Harlow: **Henryk should be glad you're on his side. I'll keep digging.**

I wasn't sure Henryk would be all that thrilled to have me on his side. Especially if we found something. Harlow seemed to think it was a great idea. But she worked for the tabloids for fifteen years before Henryk had hired her for the royal press correspondent. Actually, it was more like he'd bribed her than hired her. Semantics, in my opinion. I just hope Henryk felt the same way about what I was doing.

The queen seemed awfully concerned about the line of succession and pedigree, or whatever it was rich people called family history. I wouldn't know. None of that shit had ever mattered to me. Maybe if I had a family of my own, I would know—or care—but I doubt it. I would still be a blue-collar guy with the calluses on my hands to prove it. The only reason I gave one iota about any of that garbage was because of Henryk. In his world it mattered.

And if we were going to be a part of that world, it had to matter to us. Unless I could convince the queen otherwise.

CHAPTER 8

ERIN

Two days down and twelve to go. Anxiety buzzed beneath the surface of my skin like a swarm of angry bees. Despite all our resources, we weren't any closer to finding a way to break the marriage contract Henryk's parents had arranged with Posy's. If we didn't do something and soon, I was going to be filling out my R.S.V.P. card for the royal wedding with a plus two. The thought ratcheted up my anxiety even more, tightening my chest and throat until I felt like I was going to throw up or pass out.

Desperate for fresh air, I abandoned my tea and marched across the opulent guest sweet and headed to the patio, pushing the French doors open wide as I stepped onto the stone slab. This wing of the castle overlooked the expansive garden, complete with reflecting pool and hedge maze. With another week or two left of spring, green was still the dominant color, but based on the buds waiting to open, I knew it wouldn't be long before it was awash in vibrant colors.

Just in time for Henryk and Posy's wedding.

I pushed that thought from my mind and tried to focus on the life and beauty around me, the array of pinks, reds, and yellows that would provide a gorgeous contrast to the deep green foliage and bright blues of the sky. My heart rate slowed to something close to normal, and my chest eased enough that I could drag in a deep breath of the clean, crisp air. I was finally starting to relax, the tension easing from cramped and coiled muscles when Viktor and Silas trampled all over my Zen state of mind with a barrage of questions about my well-being from the doorway.

My lips parted in an ironic smile, and I let out a matching chuckle. "I'm fine. I just needed a minute to clear my head. It's a lot, you know? And I was just starting to feel so helpless."

"Just?" Silas asked, joining me out on the balcony. He rested his palm against the flat of my back, brushing soothing strokes with his thumb. "I've been feeling helpless pretty much since the queen announced the wedding date."

"Smooth, buddy." Viktor saddled up to the railing beside me, his gaze fixed on me as if he was completely unaware of the natural beauty all around us. "What he meant to say is that we still have time to figure this out. And we will figure it out, okay?"

The confidence in his voice belied the flicker of doubt I saw in his eyes. He wanted to believe it, he almost believed it… but the seed was planted. And once that doubt took root, it was hard as hell to pull it out. Something I know all about. It had been eating at me ever since we returned to Liechtenstein and had only gotten worse since the royal dinner.

To make matters worse, we were supposed to be attending some sort of pre-wedding ball. Just one of many celebrations leading up to the actual ceremony. If I didn't know better, I would think the queen was trying to indoctrinate Henryk, convincing him that he loved Posy and wanted to marry her one stupid event at a time until the day of the wedding.

Actually, that sounded exactly like something the queen would do.

Viktor and Silas moved closer, pressing their bodies to either side of mine, and wrapped their arms around me. Sandwiched between them, I couldn't help but bask in their warmth and steal some of their strength. I always felt better when I was with them. Safe, secure and loved.

"Thanks." I eased up on tiptoes, and turned slightly on the balls of my feet, keeping my body between them, but enough to face Viktor and give him a tender kiss. His tongue slid across my lower lip, begging for entrance, but I pulled back rather than deepened the kiss, and turned to give Silas a kiss as well. "Now that I have you, I don't want to let you go. Of any of you. There's no way I could get through this without you."

I wanted them to hear how much they meant to me. To know what was in my mind and heart. Of course, they knew how I felt about them. The same way I knew they felt about me. It was impossible not to pick up on something like that whenever we were together. Each touch, each caress showed what was truly in their hearts. Whether it was the soft and tender caress of devotion, or the rush of passion that left my skin and soul on fire.

We laid ourselves bare in more ways than one.

But for some reason, right now, it was important for me to tell them how much I needed them. For them to hear the words permanently imprinted on my heart and mind. On my soul.

"I love you both." I shifted my gaze between them and took Viktor's right and Silas's left hand in mine, lacing our fingers together. "So much that my body feels full to bursting, that it isn't possible to hold another ounce beyond what I feel for the three of you. Whatever happens, I can't…Just promise me you won't leave me. That you'll stay with me."

Viktor slipped his hand from mine and gripped my shoulders, turning me so that my front was pressed against him with Silas at my back. Viktor leaned in, his breath a warm caress as he whispered in my ear, "Always." He nipped my earlobe and marked a trail of fire with each kiss along the length of my neck.

"Forever." Silas's breath was heavy with emotion and desire. He nuzzled against the other side of my neck and kissed his way down to my shoulder, where his teeth grazed my skin with promises of things to come.

This felt right, being with them, and yet it wasn't. Something was missing. Viktor and Silas would help me pick up the pieces if I had to give up Henryk, the same way that I would for them. The love we shared would get us through losing our prince.

I'd be content, if not complete.

"Come on, we have a ball to get ready for." Silas squeezed my hand and gently pulled me away from Viktor, leading me off the balcony and back into the suite.

"Now? The ball is hours away. We have plenty of time." I reached for Viktor, missing his touch immediately and needing to hold onto him.

He took my hand, the third link in our chain, and followed us inside. "Good. Silas and I plan to use every minute of it, starting with drawing you a bath."

Silas led us into the bathroom, which was larger than the studio apartment I leased back home. Everything was either white marble or white porcelain with fittings and fixtures in gold finish. Vases with fresh cut white roses occupied a space on the solid marble countertop between the his-and-hers sinks. Another bouquet of roses and baby's breath sat on the white vanity table beside a hairbrush with a gold handle and matching comb.

Viktor filled the deep soaker tub with hot water, perusing the selection of oils and bath salts on a mirrored tray on the tub's ledge before making his selection and pouring a generous amount into the bath. He turned off the faucet and moved to the counter, removing two roses from the vase, and proceeded to pluck the petals and scatter them across the surface of the water.

They took their time undressing me, worshiping every inch of my skin the moment it was exposed, and guided me to the tub where I submerged myself in the steamy, vanilla scented water. My skin was flushed, not only from the temperature of the bath, but from the sight of Viktor and Silas removing their clothes as they prepared to join me.

Silas stepped into the tub and sank down behind me, straddling his legs around my hips and wrapping his arm around me, pulling me back against the hard plane of his chiseled body. Viktor joined us, and eased down in front of me, his legs outstretched on either side of me on top of Silas's. A wicked smile tugged at his lips, all too aware of what the sight of him naked did to me.

Viktor lathered up one of those mesh netted loofahs with vanilla-scented body wash and took my hand, gently scrubbing his way up my shoulder and across my chest. The mesh grazed my nipple, barely exposed over the surface over the water, and I gasped at the friction. I arched my back, heat pooling between my legs as he swirled the sudsy loofah over one breast and then the other.

Silas moved his hand along my ribs, lower down my abdomen, before diving between my legs and gliding his fingers over my clit. He slipped two fingers inside me, the pressure of his palm adding another delicious layer to the sensation. He picked up the pace, thrusting his fingers, faster, harder, as he pushed me to the edge. Viktor cupped my breast and rolled my hardened nipple between his thumb and index finger and squeezed, easing back just before the pleasure crossed to pain. My muscles clenched around Silas's fingers, and the orgasm rips through my body.

"A girl could get used to this." The truth was, I already had. My muscles relaxed, and the coiled tension that had built up over the last few days left my body.

"Good, because we plan on doing this" —Viktor leaned in and brushed his lips across mine— "for as long as you'll have us."

Forever. I was keeping them forever. I needed them like I needed oxygen to breathe—including Henryk. I just need to find a way to keep him too.

CHAPTER 9

ERIN

I had no idea getting clean could be so dirty. Or how thorough Viktor and Silas would be in their efforts to make sure not so much as a speck of dirt could be found anywhere on my body. And I meant anywhere. I was both relaxed and exhausted, wanting nothing more than to curl up in bed with the both of them.

And our prince.

Henryk was absconded by one of the queen's advisors first thing this morning and we haven't seen him since. I missed the sound of his voice, the smile on his lips and in his eyes. The way he let us delve beneath the royal air around him, through the shyness just underneath, and draw out the passion he buried deep down inside.

Seeing him was the only part of the ball that I was looking forward to. My anxiety crept in, swirling questions through my mind and new things for me to worry about. Would he acknowledge us as more than childhood friends? Perhaps ignore us altogether? Would he ask me to dance? Would he be forced to say no if I ask him to dance? I'd never been to a real ball, and I didn't know the rules about how to behave around dukes and duchesses or lords and ladies. The last formal I attended was my senior prom.

At least the dress I was wearing tonight was definitely a step above.

Tiered layers of navy-blue tulle hung from the cascade from the hanger on the back of the bathroom door. Tiny crystals adorning the fabric added just the right amount of shimmer. The same glittering tulle wrapped around the sweetheart neckline, which plunged just enough to accentuate my cleavage to draw the eye without turning heads. A built-in bra gave much needed support to the spaghetti straps. The back curved down almost to the base of my spine, leaving my back exposed. Matching strappy heels and clutch purse completed my look for the evening.

Or so I thought.

There was a soft knock at the door before Silas peeked his head inside. "You look amazing."

"I haven't even started getting ready yet." I gestured to my makeup bag and its contents scattered across the countertop.

"That's a lot of money wasted on the counter." He smiled at my scrunched-up, confused expression. "You don't need any of the crap. You're gorgeous without it."

My heart swelled with the compliment every woman wanted to hear… or at least this one. It was nice to know that natural was beautiful. That I didn't need to change a thing about my appearance, not even a shade of lipstick, to impress him.

"Here." Silas pushed open the bathroom door and held out a rectangular black velvet box. 'This is for you."

"Silas," I gasped, reaching for the box I assumed contained jewelry from its shape and size. "You shouldn't have."

"I didn't." He chuckled before letting out a low whistle. "Henryk did, and that must have cost a pretty penny. It matches your eyes. How many carats is that thing anyway?"

Inside the box, draped over a velvet liner was the largest sapphire pendant ringed in diamonds that I'd ever seen. Light caught on the gemstone, bringing it to life with a fiery brilliance in its blue depths. I not sure I agreed with Silas about it matching my eyes. They're blue, very blue, but they have nothing on the stone dangling from a platinum chain. There are a pair of matching earrings, a ring and a bracelet to complete the set. My hand trembled as I fingered the chain, afraid I'd break it if I took it out of the box.

"Here, let me help you." Silas lifted the necklace out of its cushion, unhooked the clasp, stepped behind me, reached around me and fastened it around my neck. He brushed a kiss behind my ear. "You don't need this either. Finish getting ready. Viktor and I will be waiting to escort you."

"I can't wait to see you both in your tuxedos." Visions of us at our own wedding flashed through my mind, and I couldn't help but smile… because Henryk was there too.

It was only a dream. My perfect fantasy. One I fully intended on making a reality.

After curling, twirling and pinning my hair up on top of my head, I applied my makeup, slipped into the dress, and did a little spin in front of the mirror, giving myself the final once over from as many angles as I could. I saved the strappy heels for the last minute, hoping to spare my feet for as long as possible.

As promised, two of my favorite men were waiting for me in the living room, looking sexy as sin. The tuxedos were identical, but the custom tailoring accentuated the subtle differences in their physiques.

"How did I get so lucky?" I realized that a life with just Viktor and Silas would be more than contentment. It would be happiness. Not in the same way it would be if Henryk was with us… No. Not if, when. I made a promise to myself, to Viktor, Silas and Henryk to stop thinking this way.

"That's our line." Viktor smiled and stepped up beside me, slipping his arm through mine. "You look incredible in that dress. I can't wait to get you out of it."

"I know that look." Silas laughed and slipped his arm through mine, answering his best friend's unspoken question that was written all over his face. "That look. The one that says you're about to ravish her. And while I wholeheartedly agree with that plan, we have a party to crash and a prince to rescue."

"You can't crash a party if you're invited." Viktor shook his head and took the first step toward, leading us out of the guest suite.

The castle's ballroom was already bustling with people. The royal staff performed an elegant dance as they maneuvered the crowd, carrying trays laden with champagne flutes filled with the bubbling wine and a multitude of bite sized delicacies. Such grace and skill, and they were all but invisible to the guests. It was the closest thing to a ballet that I'd ever witnessed. Hopefully, the queen appreciated their talent and dedication. It was hard work and not for everyone. I repressed a shudder as I recalled my short-lived stint as a server for a catering company in college. Didn't last a month.

The women were all dressed in elegant gowns, adorned with jewelry that probably cost more than I've earned or will ever earn in my lifetime. The men all wore black tuxedos, some with sashes draped over one shoulder, the colors signifying their country and station. World leaders, dignitaries, royalty from other nations, and even celebrities had secured and accepted their invitation to the ball. The amount of wealth and power in this one room was staggering.

I am so out of my league.

Viktor and Silas stayed by my side, guiding me through the sea of famous, powerful people until we found a quiet spot on the sidelines where we ogled the rich and famous unnoticed.

"I feel a little like Cinderella, right now." My fingers found their way to the chain around my neck, trailing their way down to the massive sapphire resting just above my cleavage.

A gift from one of my Prince Charming's, but the only one who was actually a prince.

"You'll have a happily ever after, Erin. Silas and I will make sure of it." Viktor stole a kiss, careful not to smudge my lipstick, and trailed his fingers down my arm while his best friend watched on with desire and love swirling in his eyes in an unspoken promise.

"Hope for the best, prepare for the worst, right?" I offered a meager smile and raised the champagne flute to my lips for a tiny sip, gripping the stem so tightly, I worried it would snap in my hand.

"Henryk doesn't want this any more than we do. We need to trust him. He'll figure something out." Silas rubbed comforting circles over my back, down my spine, his fingers dangerously close to slipping beneath the low scoop of the gown.

The royal herald stood at the top of the stairs and he'd almost completed the introductions. I wasn't as enamored with the royal family as the rest of the guests. I'd been in the company of the king, queen and second prince. Let's just say the crown jewels have lost their shine as far I was concerned. Nicky made his entrance and their royal highnesses followed. I was assuming it wasn't customary for them to be announced before anyone else, but this was a special occasion.

For Henryk.

"Prince Henryk of Liechtenstein and Princess Posy of Luxemburg." The herald announced them, making way for their entrance into the adoring crowd below.

The attendees gathered to celebrate their union, one to strengthen and solidify their countries and economies. The queen didn't care about love or happiness, at least not for Henryk. She wanted what she believed was best for their country, their people. Love would come in time. *It's your duty.* Henryk shared her so-called words of encouragement the last time we saw him. It had only been a day, but it felt like an eternity since we were all together.

Was this what it would be like if we stayed with Henryk? Secret lovers pining for a moment alone with their prince? Stolen moments?

"May I have this dance?" Nicky extended his hand and an invitation to join him on the dance floor for a waltz. Mischief shimmered in his eyes. He was probably scheming up another plot to destroy Henryk... again.

"Of course," I accepted, clenching my teeth and forcing a smile on my face. There were too many people watching to refuse him.

Nicky kept a feather-light touch on my hand as he led me out onto the dance floor. The couples, clapping for the orchestra as the last waltz completed, parted to make room for the prince, second in line for the throne. Nicky looked like Henryk, a younger, softer version of the prince who stole my heart. But they were nothing alike. Henryk was filled with a quiet confidence. He was graceful, generous with his time and heart, but more importantly he was a loyalist—duty and honor-bound to his country. Nicky on the other hand, oozed playful arrogance. His place in the line of succession afforded him certain luxuries with his public persona that weren't afforded to his older brother.

Which was why Henryk's love affair with me, Viktor and Silas was so scandalous.

The music began, and Nicky took the lead, navigating our way across the dance floor. He held one of my hands in his, while his other rested on the small of my back, pressing us together. He leaned in, his mouth close to my ear, giving voice to all my fears over losing Henryk.

"The princess is radiant tonight, don't you think?" He was goading me, trying to make me jealous and rile me up, but I knew Posy wasn't interested in Henryk that way.

Not that facts would stop her from fulfilling her duty and marrying him if she has to.

Nicky didn't let up. "They're such a beautiful couple. Imagine what their children will look like."

My heart stopped and then stuttered back to life with a painful thump in my chest that rattled my ribcage. Nicky found the soft spot and drove a knife right through it. If Henryk married Posy, he'd have children with her, a family with her. Out of duty, but he'd love their children regardless.

I may have his heart, but Posy currently had his future, whether she wanted it or not. I thought about staying, about becoming his mistress because the thought of losing him was too painful, but I knew I couldn't. The idea of having to watch him raise a family with another woman…I couldn't

God, everything hurt. My heart, my mind, my soul. It felt like I was being ripped into a thousand pieces. I couldn't think, couldn't breathe, and I just wanted this fucking dance to end. For Nicky to shut his venomous mouth and remove his wandering hand from my back.

"Will you be his mistress, Erin? Will you let him take you with the scent of his queen's arousal still clinging to his skin, only to leave your sheets cold, your bed empty each night he returns to hers." The press of his body against mine, the feel of his arousal as he offered to make me forget Henryk made my stomach roil. "Perhaps I could warm your sheets on those cold, lonely nights. I promise you'll enjoy it. You'll forget all about Henryk. I've done my research. I know how to please you."

He'd done his research? Oh, God, the drone footage. He'd watched it. And more than once. Champagne and caviar threatened to make their way back up, but I couldn't make a scene. I wouldn't embarrass Henryk.

The orchestra was winding down. I could do this. I have to do this. As soon as the waltz ended I'd slip out of the ball.

And out of the castle.

CHAPTER 10

HENRYK

*E*rin shined brighter than all the stairs in the sky, as if she'd fallen straight from the constellations and crashed into my life. The sapphire I hand-picked because it reminded me of her eyes hung from her graceful neck and rested just above her perfect breasts. The way she bit her bottom lip, drawing it between her teeth and into her velvet mouth, deepened my need for her and reminded me of all the wicked things she was capable of with those kissable lips. She watched the dignitaries and celebrities rub elbows around her, completely oblivious to me watching her from the top of the staircase as I awaited the announcement of my entrance.

For my engagement ball.

I descended the stairs, my feet taking each step of their own volition, the lifetime of familiarity of the staircase requiring little to no concentration. A good thing too, because my mind was focused on one thing. Her. No, not just her. Them. *Us.* Viktor and Silas were by her side, unburdened by the responsibilities of a crown or country. Unbound by the shackles of a loveless, arranged marriage. I envied them their freedom, and the time they'd spent alone with her.

The things I know they had done together in my absence.

My mind wandered to the days and nights spent in Ibiza and the day we professed our feelings—our love for Erin and each other on our deserted island. We were desperate for rescue, but I would trade all the luxuries in the castle to be back there with nothing but the three of them, where we were free to be ourselves.

"She is stunning, isn't she? If Erin wasn't already taken by three of the sexiest men in Lichtenstein, I might try to expand her horizons myself." Posy's hand was draped over my forearm and she gave it a little pinch. "My beloved and I would show her the time of her life."

"Posy!" That comment earned her a genuine laugh. While this arrangement was far from a love match, I reminded myself that at least she was my friend, and even if it wasn't a life I wanted, it would be an amicable one.

"You know, Henryk, you really do need to claim what is rightfully yours." Posy's head was fixed forward, chin up with that air of royal elegance, but I felt her watching me from the corner of her eye.

"I thought that was the point of this ridiculous ball." I didn't spare as much as a sideways glance in my fiancé's direction as we passed the receiving line, remaining the perfect prince I was before I'd brought Erin, Viktor and Silas back into my life. "And our engagement."

"With the education you had, you cannot possibly be that dense." Posy broke protocol and the emotionless mask she hid behind and glanced at me.

"Of course, not. Ray and I have a small team of royal and legal advisors working on a solution, but I dare not allow myself to hope, because losing them will be that much worse if I do."

"Oh, Henryk." She gave my arm a squeeze, and I suspected for the first time she realized the full scope of the situation that I was in.

Posy and my circumstances were similar, but not the same.

The orchestra lured the guests onto the dance floor with Strauss' Blue Danube, a familiar and classically beautiful waltz, and a personal favorite of my childhood dancing instructor. Posy and I remained seated, watching the rich, powerful and famous twirl themselves around the parquet floor as was customary, and awaited the announcement of our dance together. A preview of the one we were expected to share on the day of our wedding. The waltz came to a close, and the guests offered restrained applause, the sound of their clapping muffled by so many satin-gloved hands.

Tchaikovsky's Flower Waltz began, and my fingers ached to take Erin's hand in mine, to grip her waist as I led her on the dance floor in a white version of the dress she wore tonight, inlaid with the finest crystals to catch and reflect the light as we moved together on the dance floor. Viktor and Silas would take turns cutting in, a moment shared between the four of us. A prelude of the night that should be to come but wasn't.

Nicky stood, shattering my perfect daydream with his sudden movement, and crossed the room. What the hell was he up to now? No, he wouldn't. He couldn't possibly...but he was. He did. The fucking gall. Anger turned to rage, my pent-up frustrations fueling the fire that scorched me from the inside out. I was a dragon, flames roaring within my chest, ready to decimate my enemy—my brother— for daring to touch her after everything he'd done.

"Henryk, do not give him the show that he so desperately wants." Posy's gloved hand slipped over mine and she gave a gentle squeeze, her words momentarily banking the inferno within me.

His invitation for a dance put her under the spotlight. She gracefully accepted, not that he left her with any choice. My fingers curled around the arm of the chair. The centuries old wood protests under the strain of my grip. My teeth are clenched together but I keep the mask I wear for the public firmly in place, giving nothing away as I watch my snake of a brother dance with the woman I love.

"Remain calm, Henryk. He's goading you. It's just a dance and... Oh, no...Shit," Posy seethed through her false smile, noting the same shift in Erin's body language, in the expression on her face that I had. "Henryk, don't make a scene. We need to play the game until we are..."

She trails off, tapping the white satin encasing her fingertip against perfectly stained soft pink lips.

"Actually, forget my advice, Henryk. Listen to your heart." She offered a discreet wink and tilted her head in Erin's direction. A slight movement that no one who wasn't scrutinizing her every movement would notice, and with all eyes fixed on Erin, that was unlikely.

Follow my heart. Not the best advice, considering it beat like a wild animal with a willful mind of its own, trapped beneath my ribs, thrashing against its boney cage. The need to protect her, to rip my brother's hands from her body was overwhelming, all consuming.

Viktor and Silas seemed to notice the shift in Erin's demeanor as well. I noticed them in my peripheral vision, ready to move onto the dance floor and rescue our damsel as I rose from my seat to the very same thing. No. I caught their attention and shook my head. I needed to do this. I had to do this.

My shoulders were squared, my spine straight and my stride purposeful. I was a prince ready to do battle, to rescue his princess. And I was about to make a big fucking scene, at least where my mother was concerned. Which only made me that much more determined to do it.

I moved across the dance floor, cutting off Nicky's next step in the waltz with a forceful tap on his shoulder. The slight wince in the corner of his eyes was incredibly satisfying to the primal beast Erin had unleashed within me. "May I cut in?"

The smile on my face was for the cameras. The threat uttered between clenched teeth was for my brother. "You will remove your hands from her body. Immediately."

"Or what, brother?" Nicky sneered as he swept Erin into a low dip and leered at her breasts. He snapped her up and pressed her against him.

She said nothing. Did nothing. And I know her silence is for me. To spare me. This was why I could never allow her to be a mistress. It lessened her standing and her worth. And she was worth everything. Erin's love was a priceless treasure.

"You forgot your place, Nicky. Keep touching her and I will make a ritual of reminding you. Every day of your worthless existence." I grabbed his wrist, the one connected to the hand far too close to Erin's ass, and ripped it from her body. "Now, I think the lady is in need of refreshment. Excuse us."

"I noticed you didn't say 'my lady'." The corner of Nicky's mouth curved into a viper's grin. He struck and his poison was spreading through her veins and heading straight for her heart.

The implication of what he said was obvious in her eyes. I hadn't meant anything by it, hadn't given the choice of words any thought beyond Erin being a lady he was undeserving of. And yet, he'd found a way to twist my words in her mind.

"Shut your mouth and keep your forked tongue behind your fanged teeth." I placed my hand on the small of Erin's back and led her off the dance floor toward the gilded doors leading into the game room.

The feel of her soft, supple skin beneath my hand combined with the rise and fall of her breasts confined beneath the fabric of her dress sent a rush of blood to my groin, straining the inseam of my pants. It had only been a day and a half since we were together, but it felt like an eternity. I ushered her through the door and kicked it closed behind me.

"Erin, my love. Are you alright?" I cupped her face in my hands, searching for the truth in her eyes because I was afraid she wouldn't tell me the truth. That my brother had tainted what's between us.

She nodded her head, pulling her lush bottom lip between her teeth again, and held back the tears glistening her eyes.

"I love you, Erin. Never forget that no matter what anyone says. No matter what happens, today, tomorrow, or any day after, never doubt that. Never doubt how much you mean to me."

"Prove it." She laid the challenge at my feet with heat and passion in her eyes.

I knew what she was asking for in that moment and what she was asking for our future. I could only give her this. Anything else would be a lie, and I would never lie to her.

Hands gripping her waist, I backed her up against the wall, buried my face in her neck, and breathed in her vanilla scent. It was intoxicating. She was intoxicating. I reached beneath her the layers of tulle, ran my hands up her silky-smooth legs and gripped her bare ass. The thin layer of lace from her thong was the only thing separating her sensitive flesh from me. I wrapped her leg over my hip with my left hand and tore at the thin elastic strap, tearing the thin layer of lace away and sliding my fingers over her folds, slick with need. She was ready for me, wanted me as much as I wanted and needed her.

The door to the game room opened and closed with a soft click. I expected it to be Ray, sent to fetch me by my mother and catching me in a compromising position in the process. But it wasn't. I recognized the heady mix of their colognes and the cadence of their breathing. The little details you only come to know about a person when you've intimate with them made their presence familiar to me. And it heightened my arousal.

I want them to watch me take her right her against the wall… to make her come.

Erin called for them to join us. I could sense her need for them as well, in the hitch of her breath, the soft mewls of pleasure when they entered the room. The way she looked at them. It was the same way she looked at me.

"No, baby." Viktors answered the silent request in her outstretched arm. "This is for Henryk. We're happy to watch."

"Then watch. Watch him fuck me." She gasped when I slipped two fingers inside her, sliding them in and out. "Touch yourselves while Henryk takes me. Make yourselves come while our prince makes me come."

I loved it when she talked like that. The way she took control and told us what she wanted us to do. The dirty words that came out of her sweet, perfect mouth. It drove me crazy and pushed me nearer the edge. I was so hard, so close as it was. I knew I wouldn't be able to take my time with her. But tonight was different anyway. Tonight was about pure, unadulterated need. Raw and primal.

I unzipped my pants, pulled out my throbbing dick, and rubbed the tip over her entrance, dripping wet and ready for me. And then I was inside her with one hard thrust, burying every inch. She clutched her tulle dress, pulling it up higher to give Viktor and Silas a better view while I rocked my hips, pumping in and out of her, fucking her right there against the wall, in the castle.

Some would say this was illicit, depraved to take a woman like this in front of other people, but I loved it because I loved them. And I knew they feel the same way. Having Erin this way, with Viktor and Silas watching us, pleasuring themselves while I pleasured her, inside the castle where I was bound by rules all my life was incredible. Erotic. Freeing.

Erin came, her pussy contracting around my dick, milking me as I chased her orgasm with my own. I was still buried inside her, basking in the throbbing aftermath of a mind-blowing finish when Viktor and Silas came. It was complete. We were complete. I wanted to stay in this room with the three of them, giving and taking pleasure from one another. And I planned to do just that—at least for tonight.

But the crown had other plans.

CHAPTER 11

SILAS

Knock. Knock. Knock. Knock. Knuckles wrapped against the door hard enough to vibrate through the heavy, solid wood doors at our backs. Eyes wide, eyebrows raised, I glanced at Viktor and saw a similar expression. Surprise shifted to amusement, and I knew my satisfied smirk matched his. We were about to get caught with our pants down. Literally. In the castle, no less.

The knowledge that we could get caught, that a royal guard could walk in on us at any second just added another layer, heightening the experience of watching Henryk fuck Erin against the wall. He was like a man possessed, different from the attentive lover he normally was. It was hard and fast, but no less passionate. In fact, it was the opposite. It was passion that pinned them against that wall. An explosion of pent-up desire and need.

And it was sexy as fuck.

Watching was just as arousing as participating, especially when it was with people you loved. We watched Erin, Erin watched us. All of us were an extension of the other, sharing in each other's pleasure, feeding off it because of our deep connection to one another.

Another knock. The doorknob jiggled.

"They're not going away." Viktor chuckled, tucking himself back in and zipping his pants.

"Doesn't sound like it." I did the same, sparing a quick glance at Erin and Henryk, to make sure they were more than presentable.

Erin nodded, re-pinning the last of the curls that had fallen out of her the formal hairstyle she worked so hard on before the ball. The tousled hair just added to her sexiness. It grated on my nerves that she had to rush to fix it, as if she had to be ashamed or hide it for Henryk's sake.

Fuck that. And fuck them for making us feel that way. Like there was something wrong with the way we felt about each other.

"Your highness." Ray rushed past one of the royal guards, checking him with his shoulder as he made his way into the game room once we unlocked the door. With his back to his subordinates, he offered an apologetic smile and delivered the announcement we all knew was coming. "The queen requests your presence, sir."

I preferred the more relaxed version of Henryk's head of security. The one we befriended in Ibiza, who only got to show us his true self behind closed doors, a lot like the prince who employed him.

The guards behind Ray surveyed the room, no doubt mentally preparing a report to give to the queen after the ball. Assholes. One of them opened the other door and two more shuffled in, taking position on opposite sides of the doorway.

"Tell my mother—"

"It's okay, Henryk. You need to get back." Erin took his hand in hers. A soft, tender gesture that didn't reflect any of the passion lingering in the air. Or the way we really felt about each other. She was schooling her features, slipping an emotional mask back in place as if she had a lifetime of practice, like a royal. "Thank you for escorting me out and making sure that I'm alright. I feel much better now."

"Are you sure you are okay?" Henryk looked at her, a silent plea for a reason to stay written all over his face, swirling in his eyes. He didn't want to go back any more than we want him to leave.

But Erin gave him permission to do just that.

"I'm fine. I promise." She smiled at him, a silent reassurance that passed between them, between us, because we knew each other so intimately. "I'll stay here with Viktor and Silas for a few minutes in case I'm still feeling faint."

FROM THE WAY the portraits on the wall were rocking, Henryk had ridden Erin hard, but enough to make her faint? Weak-kneed sure. On the verge of passing out? I'm calling bullshit. Not because I didn't think the prince had it in him. Based on this performance, I'd say he certainly did, and I couldn't wait until we were all in bed together to participate in that monumental occasion, but I could hear the lie in her voice.

She was giving him an out. A cover story for why he'd swept her off the dance floor, across the ballroom and into this...whatever the hell this room filled with pool table, snooker table, roulette and poker tables, was called. All it needed was a couple of slot machines, and I could just call it a casino.

"Ray, please stay behind and escort our guests back to their room when Erin is ready while I have a word with my mother and see to Posy." His brows drew together and the muscles in his jaw twitched as if it pained him to say that last. He gave a nod to me and Viktor, something almost like an apology in the look he gave us. "Feel free to enjoy the game room while you wait, gentleman."

With that, our prince and his guards walked out of the game room.

I hated the way that sounded. Game room. It's so...rich. Pretentious. So unlike Erin, Viktor or me. Hell, even Henryk. I didn't mind the gilded ostentatiousness of the castle before. Perks like a twenty-four-hour personal chef, room service and housekeeping made the restrictions of royal life easier to overlook.

At least for a little while.

It was fun to play pretend. To extend the vacation and our time together, but what I just witnessed—the exchange between Henryk and Erin—was making me question some things about our future together.

"Any news from Harlowe?" Viktor pressed Ray for an update on the dirt they were trying to scrounge up on Nicky in the hopes of gaining leverage with the queen, forcing her hand to stop the marriage to Posy.

Which is what we all wanted, including Posy. But what happened if we actually got what we wanted? The queen canceled the wedding, and we stayed with Henryk. Then what? I felt like I'd just caught a glimpse of that future. Henryk was still under his mother's thumb, and we were still in the shadows. Making excuses. Creating cover stories. Lying.

In a way it was easier for Erin. If the wedding was canceled, she could slip into Posy's place. A love story. Every girl's fantasy. A prince and a common girl. True love beat the monarchy, and they lived happily ever after. It played well, sold even better.

So where did that leave Viktor and me? What happened to us in the fairy tale ending? Were we still playing house behind closed doors, hiding our relationship from the cameras while we pretended to be a part of Henryk's staff? More lying.

I wanted to hash all this out with Viktor. See if he's felt the same way, or if I was just stressing over nothing. But it would have to wait until we were back in our rooms. Until Erin fell asleep. I didn't want to keep anything from her, but this was a conversation I needed to have with the person who knows me as well, if not better than my family. My best friend. My brother. I couldn't help but worry that if I shared all this with Erin, she'd misunderstand. Viktor wouldn't.

There was no sugar-coating or sparing each other's feelings. It was real talk, real shit. The truth.

Ray offered to fill us in on what little progress he and Harlowe had made digging into Nicky's background while he escorted us back to the guest wing.

"I wish I had more news to share. But don't worry, we're not giving up. Nicky's neat and tidy past has Harlowe more convinced than ever that he's hiding something. That woman is like a dog with a bone. She's not letting go of this now that she's sunk her teeth into it." Ray ushered us inside our suite and made his apologies for not being able to stay. As the head of Henryk's security and trusted confidant, his presence was needed at the prince's side.

Especially tonight.

Erin still carried a little flush in her cheeks from sex with Henryk in the game room. I loved the way she looked afterward, that post-sex glow. It's like a halo around her, revealing her for the angel she truly is.

But there was still the underlying stress and worry over Henryk and our future dimming her shine.

As much as I wanted to comfort her, I wasn't in the head space to make promises. I needed a little reassurance myself and I couldn't ask that of her. Not right now.

Viktor offered to fix a nightcap, but Erin declined. It was more than obvious tonight's extreme highs and lows had left her exhausted. She needed a good night's rest. Something that has eluded us with Henryk's absence. She slipped off her heels, padding across the room to kiss us goodnight. I loved watching the sway of her hips when she walked.

It made watching her walk toward her bedroom without us a little easier.

"I heard that." Viktor poured bourbon two fingers high into a glass for each of us. After adding one oversized ice cube to mine, he passed me the glass.

"Heard what?" I swirled the amber liquor in the glass, letting it roll over the ice cube and drop in temperature before taking a sip.

"The sigh of relief when Erin went to bed. What gives?" He took a long pull from his glass, eyeing me over the rim as he waited for me to fill the silence. "I know you want to talk about it. You know you want to talk about it. So, talk."

"That obvious, huh?" I downed the bourbon and headed to the bar for another, filling the glass to the rim.

"Dude, we've known each our whole lives. It's more than obvious, at least to me. I don't think Erin picked up on it though." Viktor took the decanter and topped off his glass.

"Yeah, I think she's too wrapped up in her own thoughts to notice anything right now." I tried to keep the bitterness out of my voice, but it was there, and I knew Viktor picked up on it.

"You're worried she's going to give up everything, choose Henryk and stay here in Lichtenstein, aren't you?" As expected, Viktor cut through the bullshit and got right to the heart of the matter.

"Yeah, maybe." I gulped down the bourbon, savoring the slow burn and warm rush of the alcohol. "Which, I mean, that's her decision, you know? I can't be mad at her for that. Who could blame her? He's a prince. He lives in a castle. A ranch with an open floor plan and a construction company can't really compete with that. So, where does that leave us?"

Swapping the glass in my hand for the bottle on the bar, I plopped on the couch and sank into the cushions, prepared to drown my sorrows with what was probably the most expensive alcohol I'd ever have in my life.

"It doesn't leave us anywhere." Viktor crash landed on the cushion beside me, propping his feet on the antique coffee table and snatched the decanter out of my hands. "We stay or we don't. That's up to us as much as Erin's choice to leave or stay is up to her."

"And you're good with that?" I rested my head on the back of the couch and stared up at the ceiling. "Because I'm not. I'm not good with any of it. This whole situation is fucked."

"Fuck no, I'm not good with any of it." Viktor took another long pull straight from the bottle of bourbon. "It's a mess. You're right about that, but I'm not giving up on Erin. Or us. And you're not either. Now, if you're done with the pity party bullshit, let's finish off this bourbon and see how many bad ideas we can come up with to solve our problems."

"I'm not giving up. I just don't want our relationship to be reduced to an affair. I don't want to be living a lie for the rest of my life, you know? But I can't walk away from Erin either."

"I know, brother. I know." Viktor nudged my shoulder with his and handed me the bourbon. "We're going to figure this out. Because I can't walk away from her any more than you can."

There was no fairy godmother waving a magic wand to fix this fairytale for us. We were going to have to make our own happily ever after, because I loved Erin too much to let her settle for anything less.

79

CHAPTER 12

HENRYK

"Have you completely lost your mind?"

My mother's shrill voice assaulted me the second I entered her office, piercing through the lingering effects of too much champagne last night—a failed attempt to get through the remainder of my engagement ball without Erin, Viktor and Silas at my side—and not enough coffee this morning.

"You've embarrassed yourself and your fiancée, but worst of all, you embarrassed your family."

She cleared her throat and smoothed the frown lines around her mouth, as if she just remembered that we weren't alone. Her royal mask was back in place. She snapped her fingers, requesting the presence of her personal assistant, who was doing her level best to blend into the wallpaper and avoid my mother's wrath. After a quick review of her itinerary for the day, she dismissed a visibly relieved staff member and refocused her attention on me.

"Tell me, Henryk, what exactly was going through your mind last night? Parading that woman across the dance floor only to disappear into one of the rooms off limits to the other guests celebrating your engagement to Posy?"

"That she needed rescuing." My calm voice and relaxed stance as I waited for her to extend the invitation to have a seat in one of the chairs opposite her belied the anger and animosity building within me.

"From whom?" She motioned for me to take a seat and poured tea into two porcelain cups. "Surely, you don't mean Nicky. Your brother would never harm that woman. Or any woman, for that matter."

"Her name is Erin, Mother." I ground out behind clenched teeth. "Do not refer to her as that woman again. She has done nothing to deserve such hostility from you. And yes, I do think my brother would harm her if it meant harming me in the process."

We were off to a bad start, and if I had any hope of smoothing things over with my mother, of changing her mind and making her see things my way, I needed to control the conversation. Something not easily done where my mother was concerned. She liked to be in charge and ensured everyone around her knew and never questioned that. Meanwhile, my father ruled from behind the curtain of my mother's skirts.

"Oh? A starring role in the most graphic sex tape scandal involving not just any member of a royal family but an heir to a throne and ruining an engagement that has been arranged since you and Posy turned sixteen is not a reason for me to feel hostility towards her?"

"A sex tape that never would have existed if not for Nicky." My fingers curled into fists on my lap as I struggled to control my temper. Shouting at my mother wouldn't help me accomplish my goals. "Ray has proof Nicky purchased the drones. The email used to send the video clips to the press has been traced back to him, and the tips to the paparazzi were Nicky's doing as well. Harlowe admitted as much."

"And you rewarded her with the most coveted position in the royal press corp." She took a sip of her preferred bergamot blend, careful not to stain the fine porcelain with lipstick, and watched me over the rim of her cup.

"I thought a king was supposed to keep his enemies close?" I offered a casual shrug and reached for my own cup of tea, adding a splash of lemon and spoonful of sugar.

"Are we enemies now, Henryk?" She set down her cup and extended her arms, reaching for me across the table.

Before Erin, Viktor and Silas walked back into my life I would have been the devoted son and prince, taking her advice whenever she gave it—which was often—and lived the life she wanted for me. It wouldn't lead to happiness, but I would have been happy to do it because that was my duty.

But now that I've had a taste of true love, of what happiness truly felt like I couldn't go back to being the man I was before. He didn't exist anymore.

I stayed in my seat, refusing to reach over the table and join hands. "It's starting to feel that way, Mother."

Her mask faltered, the emotions slipping out from behind it. Disbelief, sadness, disappointment. But there was still love underneath it all. If I could just get her to think like my mother and not like a queen, perhaps I could convince her. It was a fool's hope, but I had to try.

Because I cannot go through with this wedding.

Last night was proof enough of that for me. Watching Nicky dance with Erin, the thought of someone replacing me, a new fourth? Something broke inside me. I realized that I was worthy of love, that I deserved to be loved, and on my terms, not the crown's. My former fiancée deserved the same, and with me out of the way, perhaps she would have a chance at it as well.

"A true king doesn't keep his enemies close in the hopes of avoiding a threat. He simply removes the threat entirely." My mother rose to her feet, the points of her heels sinking into the plush carpet, and retrieved a stack of papers from her desk, each bearing the official seal of the monarchy. Clutching them to her chest, she returned to her place on the settee.

"Is that the means with which you plan to eliminate this manufactured threat?" Elbows resting on my knees, I leaned forward, all but pleading with my mother to end this before it began. I knew what she planned to do, because I came here with similar intentions, and it was clear to me that this wasn't going to end well for either of us. "Is popular public opinion worth my happiness? The life I want is nothing we don't already permit for our own citizens."

"Then you can live among them, Henryk." She set the stack of papers on the table beside the tea service. "If that is what you wish."

"What I wish for is the support of my mother. That she would look beyond the crest and crown and into her heart and choose her son for once." I pushed off the couch and stormed across the room, snatching the gold pen from her desk. "Threatening me with my freedom was a miscalculation on your part, Your Highness."

"I can see that." She turned in her seat, watching me over the back of the couch. Her lips mashed into a thin line, and scowl lines erased years of a strict skin regimen, and marred her wrinkle-free skin. "Still, I am prepared to follow through with it. The question that remains is, are you willing to live with the repercussions of your actions?"

"You mean being happy? Living my life with the people I love? Those repercussions?" I reached for the papers. "If the choice is to marry Posy and secure my place as heir or give up my claim and be free to live with Erin, Viktor and Silas, then my choice is easy. I choose love, Mother. I choose love. Where do I sign?"

"Henryk." She gripped the stack of papers in her hand, white-knuckled, with a look of disbelief on her regal face. "You would really do this? Turn your back on your responsibilities?"

Now was not the time to hesitate. If I stopped to think about the possibilities, the ramifications of my actions, I would lose all my nerve and cave to the pressure of the crown. Like every other day and decision of my life. Not once had I put myself first. A leader, a king, must be selfless, not selfish. A lesson I was taught right alongside reading and arithmetic.

That was about to change.

For once, I would put my happiness first and foremost. It was my life and it should be my decision whom I would marry. Or who I don't. Whomever I spend my life with deserved my whole heart, and I couldn't give that to Posy because it belonged to someone else. To three someone's.

Not that Posy wanted or needed my love anyway. Our arranged

marriage was a shackle around her ankle just as much as mine. If I refused and broke the marriage contract, I wasn't the only one gaining their freedom.

"Give me the papers, Your Highness." Bitterness dripped from every word. I couldn't help or hide the anger or pain I felt over her refusal to separate herself from her position long enough to be the mother I needed her to be.

"Henryk, please. I only want what is best for you." Her hand was unsteady, the stack of papers trembling as she passed them to me.

"No, you want what you think is best for the monarchy and for the country. What is best for me is secondary. It always has been."

Pen in hand, I took the papers and signed my name on the line, revoking my claim to the throne of Liechtenstein. I was no longer Prince Henryk, heir apparent. It was the end of my life as I knew it.

It's also the beginning.

The possibilities were as terrifying as they were endless. I let my heart rule my head and chose a future not only for myself but for Erin, Viktor and Silas. I chose for them the same way my mother chose for me. Will they want a pauper in place of their prince? There was only one way to find out.

CHAPTER 13

ERIN

I didn't mean to eavesdrop on Silas and Viktor last night. After everything that happened at the ball, I'd planned on stripping out of my gown and calling it a night. I was exhausted mentally and physically. At least the last part had been in a good way. Sex with Henryk had been as raw and passionate as it had been unexpected. Having Viktor and Silas there with us, watching, added another layer of excitement. It was incredible and yet somehow left me wanting. Restless. Which is how I stumbled out of my room and into a conversation between Silas and Viktor.

They were worried about the future—our future—and what that would look like without Henryk in it. I wasn't sure what I could say or do to make them feel better. How could I reassure them when I was feeling exactly the same way?

To my relief, they were still sleeping off the bourbon on the couch as I tiptoed out of my room and into the kitchenette to start a pot of coffee. A quick glance at the clock told me that one of the royal staff would be soon arriving with breakfast. Room service was one of the few perks of living in a castle that I could get used to.

Sneaking around for a quick romp in the game room with Henryk, however, was not.

The reason why last night left me feeling so unsatisfied, despite the mind-blowing orgasm, raced through my mind, distracting me from the task at hand. Water ran off the countertop onto the floor, and I was standing in a puddle before I realized I was pouring it onto the counter and missing the coffeemaker entirely.

"Damn it." I cursed myself and my stupidity, grabbed a dish towel, mopped up my mess and tossed the soaked terrycloth in the small stainless sink.

"You okay?" Viktor padded barefoot into the kitchen, rubbing the sleep from his eyes. "Here, let me help."

He swooped in and took over making the coffee while I got mugs from the cabinet and creamer from the small fridge.

"You want to talk about it?" He leaned against the counter, tuxedo pants hanging low on his hips, wrinkled white dress shirt unbuttoned and arms crossed over his chest.

Any other day the sight of him like that would be a welcome distraction, but the remnants of his tux were just a reminder of last night.

"Not particularly." I was too stuck in my head, in my feelings about what happened with Henryk, to talk about it. It was too soon. I needed time to process it or risk saying the wrong thing, something that might hurt Viktor or Silas, who was stirring on the couch.

"I'm a good listener." Viktor put on an easy smile and spared a glance at his best friend and my lover stretching stiff muscles on the couch. "Just ask Silas."

"I don't need to ask Silas." I gripped the counter, fingers curling around the lip, as I held on for support. "I heard the two of you talking last night."

Silas walked up behind me, wrapped his arms around my waist, and pressed his body against mine. He leaned in, the warmth of his breath skating across my skin as he nuzzled his face against the crook of my neck.

"I'm sorry if anything you overheard last night upset you." He pressed a kiss against the sensitive spot behind my ear. "I hope you know I would never do or say anything to intentionally hurt you. I just needed to work through a few things with Viktor and get my head straight."

"That's not why I'm upset." I let out a deep sigh, exhaling my frustrations and the thoughts darkening my mood. "Last night, what I felt in the moment was…it was amazing. But this morning…I feel…I don't know. Dirty? Cheap? Like the other woman. I know he couldn't stay. I gave him an excuse to leave, and I knew it would be like this. So why do I feel so shitty?"

"Because you want more." Viktor peeled my fingers from the counter and took my hands in his, turning me in Silas' arms until I was facing him. "Because you deserve more. Erin. Listen, I know that it won't be the same if Henryk isn't with us, but Silas and I aren't going anywhere. We want to be with you, spend our lives taking care of your every want and need."

"If you want us." Silas' arms tighten around my waist, as if he was afraid I'd slip out of the embrace and out of his life.

"Of course, I want you. I can't imagine my life without either of you in it anymore. It's just…I just…" My voice broke, unable to form the sound of Henryk's name, and I barely held back the tears threatening to spill over my lashes.

"I know, baby." Viktor leaned in and pressed a tender kiss on my forehead before pulling both Silas and me into his arms.

We were standing there, wrapped in each other's warmth, comforting each other when a knock at the door forced us apart. I headed for the door, assuming a member of the royal staff was on the other side delivering breakfast, with Viktor and Silas trailing behind me. The door swung open, stopping us in our tracks beside the couch.

"Good morning it's me." Henryk called out as he rushed in, nearly missing us in his hurried state heading for the bedrooms. He seemed to catch a glimpse of us in his peripheral vison and pivoted. "I need to talk…Oh, good. You're awake. We need to talk. I have something I have to tell you."

I had something to tell him too.

Viktor and Silas didn't know what I was about to say either. I knew they'd support any decision I made. Especially this one. A decision I made only moments before, wrapped in their arms, soothing each other in the little kitchenette. Still, I would have liked to talk to them about it, but I didn't have time. If I didn't say what I had to say to Henryk, right here, right now, I may lose my nerve. My love for Henryk would make me weak and I might give in. And I couldn't. I had to say it.

It was now or never.

"I can't do this, Henryk. I'm going home with Viktor and Silas." I blurted it out, the words tumbling over one another as they fell from my lips.

"I gave up my claim to the throne… my title, all of it. I don't want it if I can't have all of you with me. At my side." Henryk's voice was louder, carrying more excitement and drowning mine out.

"You did what?" Viktor and Silas asked almost in unison, standing wide-eyed and stock-still in the living room.

Henryk ignored them, focusing all his attention on me. He was standing close enough that he couldn't have missed what I'd said.

"Erin?" The excitement and happiness drained from his face. Pain flashes in his eyes and his skin pales. "What did you just say?"

"It doesn't matter." I waved it off, as if I could erase the words with a slice of my hand through the air. "Not after—"

"You're leaving with them?" Henryk almost recoiled, as if the thought of my leaving with Viktor and Silas caused him physical pain.

As much as I wanted to take back what I'd said, I couldn't. The words were out there now, and they'd had an impact. I knew he would be upset, that he would hate hearing what I had to say as much I hated saying it, but I had to do it. Or at least I thought I had. But none of that mattered now. Henryk was ours. He gave up everything for us, and now I needed to do some serious damage control before we lost him again.

"I was, yes." I took a couple tentative steps toward him, closing some of the distance between us. He looked so fragile, so scared that I was afraid if I rushed toward him, he'd bolt. "I didn't think I could stay here anymore, feeling like the other woman. I just needed to wait for you somewhere else, Henryk. And I would, for as long as it took. No one could ever take your place. I just…I just couldn't be here if I wasn't with you. Really with you. It was too much. I love you too much for that. We all do. Did you mean it? What you said? You gave up the crown so we can be together?"

Some of the tension eased from his body, and a spark of hope ignited in his eyes. "For a moment, I thought I was too late."

"You could never be too late, Henryk." I opened my arms to him as he walked toward me, desperate to hold him in my arms, to let him feel the love I had for him.

He dropped to his knees, wrapped his arms around my waist, and pressed his face against my stomach. Tears soaked through my pajama top, the wet silk sending a chill across my skin. I combed my fingers through his hair, stroking him, soothing him as he let the emotions bottled inside of him pour out. Viktor and Silas joined us, kneeling on either side of Henryk, resting their heads on his shoulders, arms draped over his back completing our embrace.

Henryk chose us. My mind was reeling. I couldn't believe this was actually happening. It felt like a dream that I was going to wake from at any second. Except he was still here in our arms. And we were not ever letting him go.

"So, when do we leave?" Silas pulled back from our embrace, the excitement at finally heading back to the States obvious in the smile plastered on his face.

"I think we need to decide where we're going first." I slipped my hands under Henryk's chin, tilting his face until he met my gaze. "Are you ready to leave Liechtenstein?"

We'd been so focused on stopping the wedding and keeping Henryk with us that we hadn't put any thought into what came after. Viktor and Silas had their construction company. I had my career in marketing and a firm that was expecting me to return to work, joining a team handling a major account at the client's request. Henryk was the one leaving everything and everyone he's ever loved behind. His family, his home, his country, and the only work he'd ever known—being a prince.

"I'll follow the three of you to the ends of the Earth." Henryk slid my hand in front of his mouth and kissed my palm, never breaking eye contact. "Through all nine circles of Hell. Where we are isn't important so long as I'm with you."

"Good, so Los Alamos shouldn't be a problem then. Viktor and I have that new development deal, and we need to break ground asap if we're going to make the first inspection deadline." Silas teased as he headed to the bedroom to start packing. "We should probably get going before the queen changes her mind."

"The paperwork has been signed, there is no changing her mind. Or mine." Henryk got to his feet, still holding my hand like he was afraid to let go of me and linked our fingers together. "But I agree. The sooner we get out of here, the better. Now, where exactly is Los Alamos?"

"New Mexico. I hope you have shorts because the weather is a lot different than Liechtenstein. If not, we'll just have to go shopping." I smiled and gave his hand a reassuring squeeze.

That would make two of us, because the weather in New Mexico was a lot different than North Carolina too. I had plenty of lightweight clothes at home that were perfect for the sweltering city summers. But nowhere near enough for living in Los Alamos. Living in the desert? Was I really considering moving my entire life? I could work remotely for now. Viktor and Silas could get their construction project underway, and Henryk could spend some time figuring out what he wanted to do while we worked on a long-term plan.

One that worked for all of us.

In the meantime, the boys were right. We needed to get out of Liechtenstein while the getting was good.

CHAPTER 14

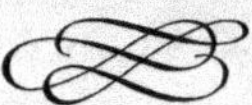

HENRYK

When I said that I would follow Erin, Viktor and Silas through the nine circles of Hell, I was speaking metaphorically. For a man born and raised in the colder, mountainous region of Europe with longer winters and cool, comfortable summers, Los Alamos was one hell of an adjustment - literally. The desert was beautiful but could have easily served as inspiration for Dante's Inferno, at least as far as the weather was concerned. The culture and people, however, were quite lovely.

Current company included.

"Henryk, are you alright?" Erin set a pitcher of lemonade in front of me on the glass patio table. Two light lunch platters of crisp salad greens, cucumbers and ripe tomatoes with vinaigrette dressing and a scoop of chicken salad on the side rested on a plastic turquoise serving tray that she placed between us.

"How could I be anything but? I'm here with all of you. No burdens, no responsibilities. Free to be who I want, with whom I want." I smiled, hoping it doesn't falter as I forced myself to lie to the woman I love. I grabbed the lemonade and wrapped my lips around the straw, taking a long sip before my smile faltered. "This looks delicious. Thank you, my darling."

Of course, telling her that I was alright wasn't a total lie. I wanted to be with Erin, Viktor and Silas, who I could be myself with. More so than I have been with anyone else in my entire life. It was a freedom I had never known and never would have if they hadn't walked into my life on that playground all those years ago.

But I was struggling to acclimate to my new environment.

I was a former prince in a foreign country with limited skills and no real work experience. I had money from trust funds and inheritances, but it wasn't financial stability that drove my need for work. It was a sense of purpose. In Liechtenstein, I did not want for anything —money or price was no object. The royal family lived a life of extravagance, but it was also a life of servitude. As a prince, I had a purpose, a cause. Countless charitable organizations, economic and environmental projects, hospitals, schools. My time was devoted to all of them. To my people. There were never enough hours in the day. Never enough time.

Now I had too much of it.

"Hmm. Are you sure you're not lying to me? Because it would be perfectly normal if you were having a difficult time adjusting to your new life here in the States." She wedged herself between me and the round table and dropped down onto my lap. She draped her arms over my shoulders, lacing her fingers behind my neck and pressed her lips to mine in a soft kiss. "It's only been a few days. You're supposed to be settling in. Getting a feel for the area. Figuring out what you want to do with your life is going to take some time."

"I'm not used to having so much free time in my schedule. You know what they say about idle hands, but I'm sure I'll find something meaningful to do with my time." I brushed my lips against hers, nipping her bottom lip.

"Mmm, I'm sure I can come up with something meaningful for you to do right now." Erin shifts her position, grinding herself against my crotch as she swings her leg around to straddle me.

Her short skirt rode up her hips, exposing the full length of her long, well-toned legs and the barely there lace panties she was wearing. Any thoughts of the future were lost in the moment and my need for the beautiful woman on my lap.

"Honey, we're home!" Viktor called out from somewhere inside the house as he and Silas arrived for our lunch date, and they were right on time for the main course.

"Dude, we're coming home for lunch every single day." Silas kicked off his work boots and padded in his stocking feet across the patio to greet Erin properly.

He fisted his hand in her hair, tugging her head back, and pressed his mouth to hers. She opened to him, her tongue slipping between his lips, deepening the kiss as I watched. My cock hardened, twitching against her core as she pressed against me, moaning into Silas' mouth.

"My turn." Viktor was there on our left, ready to claim her mouth with his.

Erin turned to him, her lips already red and plump, and kissed him while Silas and I each worked her hardened nipples between the thin cotton of her tank top and our fingers. Her soft mewls of pleasure spurred us on. Viktor tugged her shirt until her ample breasts spilled free. He dropped to his knees, pulling a nipple into his mouth as Silas did the same on the other side. I slipped two fingers beneath her lace panties between her folds and pushed inside. Her head lolled backward, her back arching as she let out a moan that made my cock throb.

"Inside. Now." Erin was hot, wet and grinding against my hand, pushing my fingers deeper inside her as she made her demand.

Her wish was our command.

We moved to the bedroom, away from the possibility of prying eyes, paparazzi or drones. We'd been fortunate since arriving in the States not to attract attention, but we were doing our best to eliminate the risk. Which meant sex on the patio, no matter how enticing taking her outside while she straddled my lap, was not going to happen.

Location wasn't everything, at least when it came to sex with Erin, Viktor and Silas. I didn't care where we were, as long as we were together.

"Tell me what you want, my prince." Erin pushed me onto bed and climbed on top of me, rubbing her slick pussy along my cock. She used my former title as a pet name, turning it into something illicit, erotic, and gave me control over her. Over us.

"I want to feel you slide up and down my cock while Viktor takes you from behind. I want to watch you take Silas into your mouth, watch you worship him with your tongue while we're buried inside you." I grabbed her hips, raising her up until the head of my dick pushed against her entrance. I eased her down and buried my full length inside her.

Viktor positioned himself between my legs, spreading Erin's ass as he eased himself inside her. The sensation of him filling her at the same time made my cock throb. Silas knelt on the mattress above my head, stroking himself until Erin replaced his hand with her mouth, her tongue laving his glistening tip until she took him fully into her mouth.

Erin's breasts bounced as Viktor drove into her. I let him control the pace, let his thrusts slide her back and forth over my dick. Silas filled her mouth, muffling her cries of pleasure. She was close, so close, bringing me with her. I cupped her breasts, pushing them together and pulling both nipples into my mouth, licking and sucking her sensitive flesh. I could feel her throbbing around me as she fell over the edge into oblivion, coming all over me. I was undone. My dick pulsed inside her as my orgasm ripped free and I erupted inside her. Viktor was right there, picking up the pace, his hips smacking Erin's ass. I held on for dear life, tremors still racking my body as she slid along overly-sensitive skin. One final thrust and I could feel his orgasm, feel him come inside her. Silas gripped her hair, holding her head still, a rough, guttural moan escaping as he climaxed in her mouth.

Utterly spent, we collapsed in a heap on the bed, fingers lazily grazing various parts of our bodies, and basked in the afterglow for as long as we could.

"As much as I hate to say it, Viktor and I have to get back to work." Silas was the first one off the bed, dipping into the bathroom to clean up before scooping up one of the piles of clothes on the floor. "I think these are mine. Nope, never mind. Those must be mine over there."

Viktor grabbed the pile Silas abandoned and headed for the bathroom. He was in and out, cleaned up and ready to finish out his workday on the construction site. After a few goodbye kisses and promises to bring home Erin's favorite shrimp tacos for dinner, they headed back to work.

"I have a few things I need to finish up for the presentation before my video call with the client at three o'clock." Erin slipped off the bed, grabbed her clothes and chucked them in the hamper before selecting a white sundress with bright red poppies on it from the closet. "I'm going to hop in the shower quickly. Want to share the hot water?"

"There won't be anything quick about the shower if I get in there with you." My gaze roamed her perfect body as I fantasized about round two. "You might want to get in there before I make you late for your meeting."

"If I haven't already missed so much time at work already, I would take you up on that challenge." She blew me a kiss and disappeared into the bathroom, leaving me to my thoughts again.

None of which were good.

It was hard to stay positive when you're drifting in a sea of possibilities, none of which seems to have any real chance of becoming a reality. I could go public, trading on my former title and lingering celebrity status here in the States, but I'd never cared for that side of royal life. That was where Nicky shines. The life of a socialite. My focus was and still is philanthropy.

Unfortunately, charity work doesn't typically pay well.

A worthwhile cause would be more than happy to welcome me as a public face for their donation drives but would be less happy to put me on the payroll and reduce into their funds by cutting me a check. Still, there had to be something out there for me. I can't and won't be a kept man. I needed to contribute here at home and in the community.

Frustration rolling off me in waves, I grabbed the remote and channel surfed while scrolling through job search sites on my phone. As expected, philanthropist is not an in demand job. I stopped on a national cable news channel, catching up on world events that didn't have the same direct impact on my daily life now as they did a week ago.

"We have breaking news out of one of Europe's last ruling monarchies." The young female news anchor's voice took on a somber tone from the lighthearted delivery of the previous stories.

She captured my full attention with her mention of last ruling monarchies. There were only a handful left on the continent, Liechtenstein among them. Had my mother and father finally issued a formal press release about my abdication? Were they ushering in the new heir, my younger brother Nicky? I sat up, spine ramrod straight, watching the television with rapt attention.

"After suffering a major heart attack, the king of Liechtenstein has been airlifted from the palace and taken to Mason Dieu Hospital, where he is currently being treated in ICU." The reporter rambled on about minor details, the helicopter used to transport my father, the number of doctors and nurses on staff at the royal hospital who would be dedicated to treating the king, how much it would cost the taxpayers to provide the necessary surgeries and treatments, as well as the massive security detail stationed around the hospital grounds.

Nicky flashed onto the screen. A media clip of him delivering thanks to the nation for their prayers and well wishes for his father the king's, speedy recovery. This happened during a press conference in which he announced his new and more complex role, filling in for his father while he was medically unfit to carry out his duties. My blood boiled in my veins as I listened to him prattle on about his supposed responsibilities while trying to erase me from the family and eject our father from the throne while he was recovering in his hospital bed.

The queen, our mother, interjected to remind everyone that her husband, the beloved king of Liechtenstein, was doing well despite being in ICU and expected to make a full recovery according to all the wonderful physicians attending to him. Several reporters questioned my appearance, or lack thereof. Harlowe did her best to misdirect, while my mother did damage control, claiming that I was overseeing foreign policy and handling international affairs during the king's medical emergency, and would be returning to the palace as soon as possible.

Nicky fumed beside her and seized control of the press conference and the press corps with a rambling list of royal decrees he planned to enact while he was acting as the ruling authority for Liechtenstein. Decrees that would increase the royal coffers while draining funds from the hardworking citizens of our country, causing unnecessary hardship during already difficult times, all the while alienating our allies with huge tariffs on imports that our businesses and consumers relied on. Our economy was strong but small compared to other countries. Global uncertainties continued to place outside pressure on our domestic markets and exports. Our unemployment rate was among the lowest in the world but that could change with the shift of the wind in a global market. Nicky's policies would put everything at risk, both at home and with our allies abroad.

He couldn't possibly be thinking of staging a coup with policies like that, c he? Knowing my brother and his thirst for power, he most certainly was. And my father's heart attack was the perfect opportunity.

"Erin." I clicked off the tv, tossed the remote on the bed, and barged into the bathroom, delivering the awful news about my father.

And the state of my country.

So much for my new-found freedom. Duty called and crown or no crown, I was honor-bound to my father and my country to return home.

With or without my lovers.

CHAPTER 15

VIKTOR

Henryk just dropped a major bomb, nuking any chance of a future together here at home. His country was in crisis and his father, the king, was in the hospital after suffering a major heart attack. One his brother didn't seem to want their father to recover from. Not that I was surprised. Nicky wasn't very subtle when it came to his feelings about the line of succession. He'd been looking for a way to supplant Henryk from the first moment we arrived in Liechtenstein.

Even earlier, if I had to guess.

The one thing Nicky wasn't counting on was his brother coming home. Henryk had been on the phone with Ray and Harlowe all afternoon, making plans for his return flight, and a security detail for the hospital visit with his father and the press conferences to follow. The prince was back and in full on damage control mode for country and crown.

But more, to put an end to his brother's coup.

That was a royal sentiment that I could get behind. I wasn't completely sold on anything else concerning the king and queen, considering how much they disliked me, Silas and especially Erin. Something they'd made abundantly clear during our stay in the castle.

But taking down Nicky after all the trouble he'd caused us? That particular royal decree had my full support.

All I had to do is convince Henryk to inform the flight crew they'd have four passengers instead of one.

"You're not half as smart as you think you are, Gilligan, if you think we're letting you head back to Liechtenstein on your own." I threw the nickname back out there, knowing full well it would get under his skin. Mission accomplished. "Good. Now that I have your attention, the three of us are coming with you. End of discussion."

"You're right. It is the end of the discussion. There's no point in arguing about this because you're not coming with me." Henryk narrowed his gaze, daring me to continue the argument.

A challenge that I was more than happy to accept.

"You're trying to push us away. Spare us from the political family bullshit and from whatever decisions you think you have to make." I crossed my arms over my chest and tried to keep a hold on my temper and frustrations, reminding myself to tread lightly with the prince. "I get it, man. I do. But—"

"Do you? Get it?" Henryk's banked anger blazed to life, engulfing the closest target in its path—me. "You barely scratched the surface of what royal life is like. What my life is like. I've lived with the security, the publicity, the politics, since birth."

"You forgot about the villainous little brother waiting to over-throw you." I arched a brow and pressed the Nicky issue a little further. "He's gunning for you hard, Henryk. You need our help to get this situation under control. I've been working with Ray and Harlowe, and I think we're really on to something."

"Viktor." Henryk's shoulders inched down a fraction, his muscles relaxing as some of the fight drained from him, only for sadness to take up residence in the pools of his dark eyes. "I appreciate that you want to help me. No one, outside of my staff, has ever…Not even my mother…"

He cleared his throat, rested one hand on my shoulder and cupped the other along my jaw. His touch was intimate, familiar and filled with longing. It was all there in the lines of his face, still visible behind the sorrow in his eyes.

"This isn't a situation that I need to get under control, Viktor." A ghost of a sad smile wavered on his lips before he pressed them into a flat line and smoothed his features again. "This is my life, and I can't run from it. I have to live it. Just as you do yours. You and Silas have worked hard to build your company, to build a life for yourselves. You need to focus on that."

"We're good at multitasking. We can focus on you without losing sight of the business." I closed the distance between us and pulled him in for a hug.

I needed to feel the comfort of someone's arms as much as he did. No, that wasn't quite right. Not just someone, but one of them. Henryk, Erin or Silas. This was the first time I'd let anyone beside Silas get this close. I kept most people at arm's length, preferring a good time to a long time, but not only did the four of us have a history, we had a chance for a future. A future I didn't know how much I wanted until Erin and Henryk crashed back into my life.

"Besides, the project is on hold for a few weeks. Problem with the city and the zoning board. Which means you have our undivided attention. It's weird, right? Almost like the universe is trying to tell you something. You should probably listen."

"Viktor." Henryk pulled back, shaking his head. "There's no future there. That's why we left. Or have you forgotten the welcome you received at the castle? I cannot drag you back to that. Even if you are willing."

"You're right. There's no future waiting there for us." I clasped my hand on his shoulder and gave a firm, reassuring squeeze. "That doesn't mean we can't build one."

"Says the carpenter." Henryk smiled as he stepped back, pulling his phone out of his pocket, and tapped Ray's name, which claimed the first spot in his contact list. "Change of plans."

"I'm a master at building something out of nothing." I offered an easy, casual shrug and motioned between the two of us before waving my hand out toward the patio where Erin was sitting with Silas.

"This? This isn't nothing. We have the foundation for something incredible."

Henryk filled Ray in, asking him to handle the travel arrangements and notify the flight crew of the additional passengers. His head of security, trusted advisor and closest confidant, must have asked him something about the sudden change, because he closed his eyes and pinched the bridge of his nose before replying that he'd already tried to talk us—meaning me—out of coming home with him. The minor frustration etched on his face shifted, and a half smile tugged at the corner of his mouth,

"Yes, Ray. You were right." Henryk sighed, a soft exhale that said a lot about his relationship with Ray. The trust, the bond, and the test of patience that only came from someone you considered true family. He lowered his voice and headed towards the patio where Erin and Silas were waiting, motioning for me to follow him. "I am not stubborn. Determined, yes. But stubborn? I know they're not going to give up on me. I already said you were right. Just make the arrangements."

Another sigh and a chuckle before Henryk ended the call with "I'm hanging up, Ray." He swiped the red button on his screen and opened the sliding glass door to the patio.

"Pack your bags, kids. And be sure to bring clothes for cold weather." I slipped by him and snagged my laptop from Silas, closing out the streaming app and opening the business email. "I need to touch base with the permit office, the architect and the developer, to make sure there isn't anything they need from us before we head out."

"I can't believe you talked him into it." Erin hopped out of her chair and rushed over to Henryk, pulling him into a crushing hug. "I can't believe that after everything...You didn't actually think you could leave us behind. That we wouldn't be there for you? You don't get to shut us out. Not now. Not ever."

That was our girl. Erin wasn't going to let him off easy for trying to make this decision for us. He was in crisis mode and not in the condition to make major decisions about our life together. Henryk chose us, walked away from everything to be with us.

And now we were choosing him.

"We love you, Henryk, and we're going to get through this together." She leaned back enough to press her lips to his in a kiss that made all sorts of promises. Promises she'd keep because that was the type of woman she was. "We're going to figure this out. All of it."

With another kiss, this one softer, sweeter, she bounded back into the house to pack her bags for our return trip to Liechtenstein.

"What the hell were you thinking, Henryk?" Silas looked like he wanted to lay into our prince but checked himself and pulled his emotions back. "It's too late to cut and run. You had your chance, but it's too late now. You're stuck with us."

"There's a very real chance that when I get home, I will have to marry—" Henryk shook his head, the words seemingly stuck in his throat.

"Not going to happen, man." Silas pushed his chair back from the table and got to his feet, clasping Henryk on the shoulder as he headed into the house. "No way in hell is that happening."

"Can I ask a favor?" Henryk turned to me, one corner of his mouth curving up into a half smile in response to my nod. "Please don't say I told you so."

"I wasn't going to say it." I curled my hand into a fist, coughing to hide my laugh. "I might be thinking it, but that doesn't mean I'm going to say it."

"I appreciate that." Henryk's laugh was rich, full bodied and rolled through him. A little more of the tension eased from his shoulders. "Come on, we have a plane to catch.

"Yep, we sure do." I followed him into the house and made quick work of repacking my suitcase.

Look out, Liechtenstein, because here we come. The rightful heir and his entourage. And this time, we weren't backing down. This time we were claiming what was rightfully ours. A life together. A future. One that included Henryk on the throne, where he belonged.

CHAPTER 16

HENRYK

The jet hit the runway with a bump and a screech of rubber. We'd hit turbulence forty-five minutes in. It was a rough flight, and the landing wasn't any better. I unfurled Erin's white-knuckled grip from the armrest and lifted her hand to my lips, pressing a soft kiss to each of her fingertips.

"It's alright, my darling. We're fine. I told you, Francois is an experienced pilot." I traced my lips with her fingers before slipping her index finger into my mouth, rolling my tongue around it.

Her eyes blinked open, those glittering sapphire orbs staring back at me as her lips parted and a small, breathy gasp escaped her mouth.

"Better?" I asked, releasing her hand and helping her with the seatbelt.

Erin nodded and cupped my face in her hands before planting a quick, sweet kiss on my lips. "Yes, thank you." She craned her head over the back of her seat, glancing at Viktor and Silas, both still asleep, earbuds in while a low-brow comedy streamed on the screen in front of them. "I guess we should wake them up."

"As much as I hate to disturb their slumber, I need to get to the hospital and see my father."

"Of course you do." She glanced back one more time before fixing

109

her gaze on me. I can almost see the wheels turning in her mind as she formulated a plan in her head. "Call Harlowe and ask her to pick us up. I'm sure there's a lounge inside the airport where the three of us can wait."

"I'll take you to the castle first, and—"

She raised her hand, palm out, cutting off any argument from me. "No. Ray will take you straight to the hospital to see your father. We're more than capable of getting settled into the guest suite without you, and you don't need to be worried about us or taking care of us. Your father is your first priority right now."

I opened my mouth, about to profess my love for her—for them—when she pressed her hand to my lips and declared it first.

"We love you too. Now call Harlowe." She waved over the seat, calling for Ray. "Take him to the hospital to see his dad."

Ray grabbed my bag from the overhead compartment, and I followed him down the jet's small staircase, out onto the tarmac where a black sedan equipped with the latest upgrades in personal security technology awaited us. We left Erin in charge of Viktor and Silas, confident in her promises to get everyone into a now private lounge Harlowe had secured inside the airport until the head of the royal press division arrived to escort them back to the castle.

"They'll be fine, Henryk." Ray spared a glance in the rearview mirror, watching me from behind the wheel. "Focus on your father. That's enough for one man to worry about for the moment. Everything else can wait until we get back from the hospital."

"You're invaluable to me, Ray. I hope you know that."

I tore myself away from his watchful gaze and stared out the window, choking back the emotions threatening to escape from the well-organized and tightly-contained boxes I normally compartmentalized them in. The stress of everything happening so fast with my title, my lovers, my country and my father were overwhelming.

News of my arrival hit the wires sooner than I had hoped. A throng of reporters and a crowd of supporters was already waiting for me, bulbs flashing as they snapped picture after picture of the car pulling into the hospital's garage. We decided against stopping outside the hospital and using the entrance reserved for the royal family, opting for a secure and private entrance through the garage. Speaking to the press in my current state of dishevelment and distress was the publicity equivalent of swimming with great white sharks while there was fresh chum in the water.

Neither was a good idea.

Ray parked in a spot reserved for clergy, turned off the engine with the press of a button and got out of the car. He walked around to the rear passenger door, opened it and stepped to the side so I was able to exit the vehicle. "Ready, Henryk?"

I nodded and followed him through the automatic doors, down a long corridor that smelled of antiseptic and something else I can never seem to place, that unusual scent found only in hospitals. We turned left down another corridor, stopping halfway down at a set of elevators. Ray pushed the button for the fourth floor. The ICU.

Machines beeped, sensible, rubber soled shoes squeaked against the tile floor as nurses and doctors shuffled from one room to the next. We navigated the hall, dodging right or left to allow nurses steering gurneys and the patients lying on them room to pass.

My father's room was heavily guarded. The two members of his security team stationed on either side of the door nodded upon my approach and opened the door. He was alone. I exhaled the breath I didn't realize I was holding. I wasn't in the mood to deal with my mother or my brother.

The king, my father, looked peaceful, comfortable. The doctors and nurses here were second to none, and the medical equipment was state of the art. He was in good hands—the best. But that did little to ease my fear that he wouldn't return to the castle. To the throne. I wanted my title back, but I wasn't ready to be king. Not yet. Not like this.

"Father." I moved to the side of his bed, taking his hand in mine, holding on tighter than I should, given his frail state. But the guilt gripping my heart made it impossible to loosen the one I had on his hand. "I'm sorry."

"I'm not dead yet, Henryk. Relax." My father cracked open one eye, watching me as a smile tugged at the corner of his mouth, and squeezed my hand. "I'm going to need that back, son. You're cutting off the flow to my IV."

A laugh bubbled up, unwinding the tension and worry knotted inside me. My father had always known how to lighten my mood, to pull me out of my thoughts and bring me back to the task at hand with a light touch. Unlike my mother's firm hand. Their thoughts might align, but their approach had always been very different. The king was the face of the monarchy. The queen was the mastermind behind it.

"Now, what is it you feel the need to apologize for?" My father reached over his head for the remote that controlled the bed and pressed the button to elevate him into a sitting position.

His blue eyes seemed paler, his skin thinner, but the vitals and steady heart rhythm on the monitor mounted on the wall above his bed reassured me that he wasn't in any immediate crisis.

"Everything," I blurted out the admission, giving voice to it for the first time. Guilt had been eating away at me since I watched the news report about his condition on TV.

He was fine before I'd left. I renounced my throne and jetted off to America and he had a massive heart attack. It didn't feel like a coincidence. It felt like I'd given my father a coronary.

"Why? Did you put the cholesterol in my arteries? If anyone is responsible it's the chef and that damned irresistible Hollandaise sauce of hers." He chuckled, the jovial sound turning to a light cough, which caused him to grip the pillow resting on his stomach. "Whoever said laughter is the best medicine never had a quadruple bypass."

"The pastries may have—"

"It was cholesterol, not diabetes. Do not take dessert from me, Henryk. I am counting on you to smuggle the occasional sweet." His smile was full and bright as he patted my hand. "Now, I am not sure what the penalty will be for carrying such contraband, and I cannot help you plead your case should you be caught, but I am certain the diet your mother prepared for me violates the Geneva Convention. Justice will be on your side."

"I think I've done enough to draw her wrath. I'm not sure I want to add the trafficking of treats to my list of offenses." I collapsed in the uncomfortable armchair beside his bed. "I am sorry, Father. I can't help but feel my actions have something to do with this. The stress I put you under surely contributed."

"Henryk, I have been the ruling monarch of Liechtenstein since before you were born. If stress was going to give me a heart attack, it would have done so before now." He waved off any further argument and winked at the young, attractive nurse who popped her head in the room to check on him. "Genetics and a luxurious appetite led to my heart problems. Not you. Now your brother, on the other hand, while not trying to kill me, is certainly trying to move me out of the castle and into a retirement home."

"About Nicky—"

"You said everything you needed to say when you left." His eyes lit up, some of the darker blue returning as he looked at me. "I couldn't have been prouder of you with the way you handled your mother. Talk about a coronation. You took control of your life and chose love and happiness over the crown. Your heart and humility, Henryk, that is what makes you a king among men. So, I am asking you to reclaim your title, your place in line behind me as the true heir with your partners at your side."

"Father, I can't. I won't give them up or keep them a secret. They are…"

His words register, breaking through the argument I'd been preparing to have with my mother since I packed my bags for the return flight. My eyes burned and vision blurs from the tears welling up. I pinched myself, certain this was a dream and that I would wake up any second on the jet flying across Europe to reach my homeland.

"What did…what did you say?" I had his permission. His blessing. Still, I needed to hear him say it one more time to convince myself my ears weren't playing tricks on me.

"You have my blessing in this, Henryk. But you have your work cut out for you." He waved off my protests about my mother, the queen. "No, she has her own set of terms that must be addressed. Terms that I happen to agree with. So, keep that in mind before you try to argue against them. Your mother is not your enemy, but you will find some members of parliament are. Polygamy may be legal in our country, but that doesn't mean everyone supports it. You need allies, son. Now, be a good boy and get your father a Danish. With real cherries, not that artificial jam business. I'll know the difference."

"He'll do no such thing." My mother breezed into the room dressed in classic Chanel—her version of casual—and stopped at my father's bedside. "Unlike Nicky, you can't bribe this one."

My mother, of all people, would know.

CHAPTER 17

HENRYK

"Speaking from experience, my love?" He patted her hand resting on the bed rail, beaming at her as she placed a tender kiss on his forehead.

"More like called his bluff." She shrugged and waved her hand not tangled up in my father's. "Still, I am confident bribes will not work. No pastries for you. Right, Henryk?"

"Right, Mother." I'd never seen this side of her. Whenever Nicky or I were sick, a nurse was sent to care for us night and day. Not my mother. I wasn't aware she had a bedside manner. Though I think it's best if I kept that little observation to myself. Things have changed in the short time since I'd been gone, and I didn't want to risk the delicate blessing they were granting.

"Good boy. Now, go home. You need to get ahead of the jet lag. I want you to rest and hydrate. I'll be home for tea. We'll talk then." My mother narrowed her gaze, a calculating look in her eyes. And there she was. The queen was back. "We have much to discuss."

I wasn't sure what her conditions were, just that my father agreed with them and asked me to keep that in mind. Whatever they were, I had no doubt they had something to do with the crown and line of succession. To say I wasn't looking forward to having that talk with my mother would be a massive understatement.

Still, a blessing? It was more than I could have hoped for. Whatever her terms, I'd gladly accept them if it meant I could be with Erin, Viktor and Silas.

With a thank you and one more hug, I left my father in my mother's loving care. I was still unable to reconcile the two sides of her. Perhaps she had learned to love my father despite their arranged marriage. Perhaps that's why she had been so convinced Posy and I would have the same future.

Except Posy and I were not cut from the same royal cloth as our parents. I thought I'd been once, but that version of me, that Prince Henryk, seemed like a lifetime ago. As for Posy, she wasn't the pretty little princess everyone thought she was and I was very much looking forward to her coming out coronation.

Ray was waiting for me outside the room, ready to escort me back to the car, barking orders to other members of the security detail into the com unit he wore twenty-four-seven. "Ready. Henryk?"

"Let's go home." For the first time those words rang true. The castle had been my home in the sense that I'd lived there, a home base. Now? With the four of us together? It felt like a real home to me. Assuming they wished to live there with me, of course.

I was getting ahead of myself. I'd have to tell the others first. My family owned multiple properties, and there were several available that we could choose from. Again, getting ahead of myself. Making plans without them. Envisioning a home with them in it. Game night, ordering in, binging movies. Lying in bed together, basking in the glow of our lovemaking. I couldn't help the smile that turned up the corners of my mouth, parting my lips. I was grinning like an idiot by the time Ray pulled the Mercedes up the drive and parked it along the pea gravel semi-circle in front of the residential entrance to the palace.

"Thank you, Ray."

I bolted out of the car, not waiting for him or anyone else to open the door and escort me inside, running straight for the guest wing.

My hand was clammy, slipping on the knob as I gripped it and opened the door, rushing inside the suite, heart hammering in my chest from excitement.

"Erin, Viktor, Silas! I have to tell you something."

My shouts drew them in from the patio. I paused, my breath stolen at the sight of them. Mine. They were mine, truly and completely. I didn't need a ceremony or coronation. This was it. This was the moment, and it meant everything to me. And I hoped for them as well.

"Henryk?" Erin's bright blue eyes were wide, her mouth agape. "Are you alright? Oh my gosh, is your father alright? Did something happen at the hospital?"

"Yes, he—" I stumbled back a step with an oomph, catching her as she flung herself into my arms.

"Oh, sweetheart. I'm so sorry. Maybe we should have come. I hate that you went through any of this alone. Tell us what happened." Erin rubbed circles long my back, kneading the muscles around my shoulder blades.

Viktor and Silas came up beside us, wrapping their arms around us. "It's going to be okay, Henryk. We've got you." They whispered tender words, holding me, loving me and I was relishing in it.

Until I realized they assumed the worst.

"He gave us his blessing." The words rushed out of me. "My mother too."

"What?" The three of them pulled back at the same time, and I instantly missed their presence, the warm cocoon of their embrace enveloping me. Questions hit me from all angles, mostly singular words. There were a lot of hows, whats, and a few whys, assuming my mother had an ulterior motive. I might have been offended by their judgment of her character if I wasn't wondering the same thing myself.

My mother always had ulterior motives. She was a natural politician.

"My mother will be returning from the hospital shortly. She's asked me to meet with her to discuss the finer points of our relationship." I scanned their blank faces, unsure if they were happy with the news that we could finally be together or not. Relief washed over me when Silas cracked an inappropriate joke about the finer points that would make a queen blush, his humor once again revealing itself to break any tension or apprehension between us.

"I can't believe they gave us their blessing. I know I should be excited, but..." Erin worried at her bottom lip with her teeth. She gave a halfhearted shrug. "I don't know...I feel like I'm waiting for the other shoe to drop."

"I'm sure it will over tea." Viktor slapped his hand on my shoulder, giving a squeeze before walking towards the bar. "For now, a toast. To living life on our terms."

Or my mother's.

"On our terms." We chorused, raising the glasses Viktor poured for us. The bourbon warmed its way down my chest, into my stomach, but nothing warmed my heart like the sight of them. My loves, here with me. Where they belonged.

Ray returned with a knock on the door and pronouncements that my mother was home and ready to speak with me in the library. "Tea will be served for two." He offered an apology to Erin, Viktor and Silas on behalf of the queen and extended an invitation to dine with her this evening. After wary glances cast between them, they accepted my mother's offer and I followed my friend, confidant and the one man outside of the guest suite I trusted to have at my side... or my back.

"Tell me, do you think I am making a mistake?" I walked beside, not in front or behind him, wanting the honesty of our friendship at this moment.

"Choosing your former spouses over a new one?" Ray teased, stirring up my first memories of Erin, Viktor and Silas. "No, I don't think you're making a mistake at all, Henryk. But you need to prepare yourself for the challenges ahead. Change is never easy. Of course, nothing worthwhile ever is."

"Sage advice, my friend." I clasped him on the shoulder, feeling better for having his approval as well. "As always."

"I am wise beyond my years." Ray's naturally steely eyes softened, and a smile tugged at the corners of his mouth. There were several years between us, but he was far from an old, wise man. Any wisdom that Ray had to offer was easily given, but it was hard earned. He knocked on the library door, pushed it open, and announced my arrival before ducking back out into the hall. "Don't blindly agree to everything she says. Think over her terms, Henryk. Make sure you all can live with them.'

I nodded my thanks for that last bit of advice as well as his friendship, and took a deep breath, preparing myself for negotiations with a shrewd and calculating politician.

"Mother." I leaned in, kissing both her cheeks and claimed my seat on the soft, dark brown leather couch across from her.

"Don't be so forlorn, Henryk. You have everything you want." She reached for the teapot, pouring two cups and dropping a sugar cube in each.

"That remains to be seen." With a wry smile on my face, I accepted the delicate porcelain cup hand-painted with the royal crest and sipped my tea, watching her over the rim. Swallowing the mouthful Lady Grey blend, I placed the cup on the saucer and set them both on the coffee table between us. "There are strings attached. What did you have in mind, Mother?"

"Your children, obviously." My mother received my full attention as she broke down the future of the royal line into clinical terms. She stripped all romance, all love and even sex from securing an heir and the continuation of our bloodline.

Children hadn't crossed my mind. Not really, not in the way they should have if I expected this to work. My father had already informed me he approved of her terms, and to my surprise, I find them agreeable as well.

Apart from the lack of sex, of course.

That might be a sticking point. But if I couldn't convince Erin,

Viktor and Silas to agree to this, our future together was over before it started. I couldn't give up my throne any more than I could give up the three of them. I wanted it all.

I just hoped they did too.

CHAPTER 18

ERIN

Dinner was delightful. Well, the food and endless flow of delicious, perfectly paired wine selections, anyway. The conversation, on the other hand, left a little something to be desired. Unlike Her Majesty, I never went to a finishing school but I was pretty sure discussing your son's sex life over appetizers was considered tacky in polite society. The queen may have been taught to mind her manners, but it seemed she'd forgotten every lesson tonight.

Henryk gave us a quick rundown of her terms when he returned to the suite. Invitro, Henryk would sire two children first. Once an heir and a spare had been born, nature could take its course, meaning Viktor and Silas were free to have children with me if they wanted. I was just a regular baby making machine, apparently. It wasn't that I didn't want children with all of them, or worried that any one of them wouldn't make a good father. I wanted that, very much. And I knew in my heart of hearts they would love each child as their own and would be amazing fathers.

What I didn't want was the queen dictating how that happened.

Still, I couldn't blame her for her concerns. I was responsible for a country, for continuing a royal line, ensuring the future of the monarchy. Well, at least I wasn't before I fell in love with Henryk. I guess I was now.

If making allies in the parliament was even half as difficult as this dinner, the number of people we'd convince to support our union was going to be a lot smaller than we'd hoped. I made a mental note to ask Henryk later if there was anything Viktor, Silas and I could do to help sway people to our side. Popular opinion and the law were on our side, but sometimes the smallest group could be the loudest. We'd just have to work harder to convince them that our way of life wasn't hurting theirs. We were all free to love and live as we chose.

And that was something we should all treasure.

"Henryk, I've arranged for you to meet with several members of parliament tomorrow. Loyalists, men and women that your father assures me will stand by your side at the wedding and your coronation." The queen pulled me from my worries over the future to the more pressing matters of our present.

"Thank you, Mother. If we can secure their alliance, I'm sure the rest of the parliament will follow suit." Henryk reviewed his talking points with his mother, exuding more confidence in the meeting than I felt.

Viktor, Silas and I focused on our meals, leaving the details to Henryk and his mother... for now. If he needed our help, we'd give it, whether he wanted to accept it or not. He had our support in this and all things, and we wouldn't hesitate to remind him of that at every opportunity. I smiled to myself, realizing that the weight of any troubles we faced would be lessened when it was spread across four sets of shoulders instead of one.

"Now, on to more pleasant topics. I've spoken with the event coordinator. There are a few minor adjustments that need to be made, but she has assured me that we are on schedule for the ceremony to take place as planned. Erin, I've arranged for a fitting with the designer. There isn't time for a custom creation, but I've asked him to hold off previewing his collection until you have had an opportunity to make your selection." She raised her wine glass, tipping it in my direction before taking a sip of the semi-sweet Riesling. "I'll be joining Henryk tomorrow, but I look forward to seeing the gown you choose. Perhaps at the fitting?"

I blinked back my surprise at her offer. Not for having a wedding gown designer with his own collection at my disposal—a future queen consort can't be seen in an off the rack gown—but for her allowing me to choose my own dress. To my knowledge, Posy hadn't been given the same courtesy. It felt like a peace offering, and I was more than happy to reach out and take the olive branch she was extending.

"I'd love that." I raised my glass in turn and took a sip, savoring the crisp white wine and what felt like a major victory where the queen was concerned.

* * *

THE LAST FEW days had been a blur. Henryk was busy meeting with members of parliament and dignitaries from around the globe, assembling an arsenal of powerful political allies. The traditionalists wouldn't know what hit them if they tried to sway public opinion. Henryk's future as king was secure, regardless of their stance on a polygamous marriage, but a smooth transition when he ascended the throne was important to all of us.

I was due to meet with Jaque for the final dress fitting in half an hour, but that wasn't the only wedding detail that had me bubbling over with excitement. I'd been working on a surprise for our wedding day.

It felt like a swarm of butterflies were flitting around in my stomach. Unable to sit still, I switched between drumming my fingers over my knees and bouncing my legs. My gaze flicked back and forth from the clock to my three handsome men. Three handsome men that needed to get out of our suite so that I could continue planning my surprise.

"What are you up to?" Viktor bent over the back of the couch, nuzzled into my neck, placed a kiss on the sensitive skin, and nipped at my collarbone, sending delicious chills racing up my spine. His deep, husky chuckle at my reaction melted my insides… and my panties.

"Nothing," I replied, playfully swatting him away. As much as I would enjoy the distraction he was offering on behalf of himself, Henryk and Silas, there were only a few days before the wedding, and I didn't have a moment to spare if I wanted this surprise to go off without a hitch.

"Oh, you're definitely up to something." Silas chimed in with a wink and a devil-may-care smile that pooled heat between my legs.

When Henryk strolled in, fresh from the shower, water droplets still beaded on his skin, and a towel wrapped low over his hips, I almost caved in to their attempt to get me to reveal my secret.

"Ganging up on me, are we? Well, I'm tougher than that, boys. You can try and torture me, but you won't get me to talk." I teased before glancing at the clock—again—and reminding them that I wasn't the only one with an appointment. They're all due at the tailor in less than half an hour.

"I think we can come up with some pretty creative forms of torture in half an hour." There was a wicked glint in Viktor's eyes as he put air quotes around torture.

"I'm up for the challenge. What about you, Henryk?" Silas continued the teasing with playful innuendo, but our prince shut him down.

"As much as we would all enjoy exploiting our princess' pressure points, we really do need to leave if we're going to make our appointment." Henryk gave me a wink and leaned in to press a kiss to my forehead. "I'm looking forward to whatever surprise you have in store for us."

"Alright, shoo. Get. You're going to be late and so am I. Jacque is an artist when it comes to gowns, but his patience is thinner than his finest thread, and he has a zero-tolerance tardy policy. Which means, if you make me make him wait, I won't have a dress."

"Sweetheart, you could wear a trash bag and still look amazing." Silas leaned in to steal a quick kiss and brushed his nose up against mine before following Viktor and Henryk to the door, where they were to meet with a very eclectic, very French fashion designer.

"Pardon, Moi." Jacque barged into the room, barely visible behind a garment bag that looked like he'd crammed the Marshmallow Man inside it. "There she is, beauty naturelle. Erin, my creations pale in comparison."

His accent drew out my name, making it sound like Ehrin, and his exuberant personality matched his vibrant blue suit with pinstripe shirt and paisley handkerchief neatly tucked into the breast pocket of his jacket.

"Jacque, you're such a sweet talker." I pushed off the couch, meeting him halfway across the living room, giving air kisses and a side hug so we didn't crush the dress hidden away inside the garment bag.

"Out, gentleman." Jacque jerked his head toward the door, watching them leave with a wistful look in his eyes. "You are a lucky girl, Erin. More handsome than the models at Fashion Week. But I must confess, I don't know how you do it. Three men? I am exhausted with just one."

I laughed and took the garment bag from Jacque, my arms drooping for a moment under the full weight of the dress, which felt like it weighed more than my hatchback.

"You just have to find the right men, Jacque." I said, as if it was that easy, all too aware of how lucky I truly was.

"I found the right man, and he is more than enough for me." He raised his hands in a placating gesture, a chagrined look on his face. "Sorry, that is not what I meant. Pierre is…how would you say it…" He tapped his finger on his lips, eyes brightening when he found the adjective he was looking for. "A handful."

"Something tells me you're a very lucky man." I opened my bedroom door and hooked the hanger inside the garment bag over the top, eager to peek inside, but waiting for Jacque, who I knew was all about the reveal.

"Oui." With a determined stride, he marched over to the garment bag and pulled down the zipper. The smallest hint of lace poked out.

He clapped his hands together. "Tres magnifique, if I do say so myself. Are you ready?"

Was I? Jacque was simply asking about the dress. But the question resonated with me, hitting me in a different way, like he was asking me about my life. Was I ready for all this? I didn't even hesitate.

My answer was a resounding yes. "Absolutely."

Henryk, Viktor and Silas were mine, and I wanted the entire world to know it.

CHAPTER 19

SILAS

Everything was happening so fast. I was thrust into the limelight, had my voyeurism kink exposed in blurred out photos of me stroking my dick while Henryk took Erin from behind, been kidnapped, lost at sea, stranded on a deserted island, then rescued only to run away from the castle with Erin, Viktor and our handsome prince.

I went from living the single life, sharing a bachelor pad with my best friend and brother from another mother, to getting a divorce from a legal marriage sprung from pretend vows spoken when I was just a kid on a playground, to getting hitched all over again to the same three people all in a matter of weeks.

And I wouldn't have it any other way.

When Henryk's father, the king, had a heart attack, I knew things were going to change yet again. We couldn't stay in the States. At least, Henryk couldn't. We had a decision to make, not that it was much of a choice. I was all in. New Mexico or Liechtenstein, it didn't matter to me. There was no way I could walk away from any of them. Not now, not ever.

Which was a good thing, since we were getting married tomorrow.

My hand slipped into my pants pocket, absently rubbing the vows I'd written. Vows I won't get to say in front of the guests packing the pews of the royal family's cathedral. It didn't matter. I'd much rather say them in bed with Erin, Viktor and Henryk. There wasn't a word written on a single line of the notebook paper that was for anyone other than the three of them. Not one fucking syllable. Tomorrow, I gave them my heart, my soul, my life.

Tonight, I wanted to give them something else.

Erin swayed in and out of my view, moving from Henryk to Viktor on the balcony, a champagne flute still in her hand while she waited for me to return with a new bottle of Dom from the prince's personal stock. He had excellent taste in wine and women. So did Viktor and I.

I wasn't sure how I got so lucky. But tomorrow couldn't come fast enough. I wanted to declare my love for Erin, Viktor and Silas in front of a room filled with witnesses. Hell, I wanted to scream it from the mountain tops. I was ready to sign on the dotted line.

Of which there were several.

The amount of legal documents, contracts, prenups and lawyers involved with marrying a prince was mind numbing. Erin, Viktor and I probably should have had someone look over the stacks and stacks of paperwork before we signed our lives away, but I didn't care. I knew enough legalese from real estate and development deals, and I wasn't after Henryk's money and the only crown jewels I was interested in were not going to be on display during Henryk's coronation. At least, I hope they weren't because...awkward. Besides, the world had moved on from the so-called scandal of our romance. They wanted a love story.

If they'd actually been paying attention, they would have seen that was what was in front of them the whole time.

Tomorrow was for them, so they know and recognize we're a family. But the glitz, the glamor, the pomp and circumstance of the ceremony? The diamonds, tiaras, celebrities, royals from other countries and the paparazzi? I didn't give a shit about any of that because tomorrow night was for us. That was when I said my real vows, made my real promises.

To love and to cherish. For all the days of our lives.

And I could not wait to really start our lives together. Henryk was some kind of a genius when it came to negotiating. He managed to secure positions in his cabinet for both Viktor and me. We'd be advising on the development of and investment in impoverished nations, from clean water to infrastructure designed to withstand natural disasters and acting as goodwill ambassadors on Henryk's behalf. All while keeping our construction business in the States. The lawyers made sure to include a clause prohibiting our company from bidding on or being contracted in any way on any project outside the commercial and residential development we were already working on back home, which was more than enough for me. As long as I could still look at a blueprint and lay a foundation every once in a while, I'd be a happy guy. It was a sweetheart deal and I still couldn't believe Henryk managed to get everyone to agree.

Look out world summits, because when he hit the diplomatic scene wielding the full power of the throne of Liechtenstein, they'd sign whatever trade agreement or peace treaty he threw in front of them.

"Silas, are you coming back outside?" Erin was leaning against the patio door, her fingers wrapped around the delicate stem of a champagne glass, tipping it towards me. "I need a refill."

"I've got your refill right here." I popped the cork, careful not to drip the fizzy overflow of champagne onto the carpet as I prowled toward her.

Erin's husky giggle and the sultry look in her eyes went straight to my cock. Talk about instant hard-on. I closed in on her, claiming her mouth. The taste of strawberries and champagne on her tongue drove me wild. Visions of her naked on the lounge chair, the sparkling wine running over her body as Viktor, Henryk and I licked it off, getting drunk on her sex as much as the alcohol fueled my hunger for her. For them.

I deepened the kiss, my tongue plunging into her mouth and pressed my erection against her, eliciting a sexy little moan of pleasure from our princess-to-be. The need to touch her, grab her and toss her onto the chair overwhelmed me, and I almost dropped the bottle of Dom. That would have been a terrible waste because now that the idea was in my head, I wouldn't waste a single drop by pouring it into a glass. My next sip would be off her smooth, milky-white skin.

Breaking away from the kiss, I pulled in a shallow breath and whispered in her ear, "Strawberries and champagne go great together, but I can think of a better combination."

Viktor and Henryk must have been reading my mind, because they'd already shedded clothes while helping Erin out of hers. They had her naked and sprawled out over the lounge chair in no time at all. She opened her legs, spreading herself wide, and I was gone.

"Fuck, you're beautiful. I want the taste of this champagne and you in my mouth." I knelt down, trickling the sparkling wine over her body. I dragged my tongue along the rivulets of Dom running over her ribs, her stomach and lower, to her sweet, sweet core, sliding between her slick folds to lick her clit.

Viktor took the champagne, dripping it over her full, perfect breasts and dropped down, pulling a pert nipple into his mouth. Henryk was on her other side, licking and sucking, his hand trailing down her side, plunging two fingers inside her while I ate my fill.

"I need…Oh god, yes…more." Erin's moans and mewls of pleasure drove me wild, and I wasn't the only one.

Viktor climbed onto the lounge chair with her, cupping her breast and pinching her nipple. She ground against Henryk's fingers and my mouth, whimpering when we pulled back. Viktor shifted her on top of him, guiding himself inside her while Henryk took position between their legs, pushing the head of his dick against her ass.

I was right where I want to be, poised for her to take my dick in her mouth while I watched them fuck her into oblivion. She was magic with her mouth, and my orgasm was hot on the trail of hers. It was right there, so close. Every swirl of her tongue along my shaft, the feel of hitting the back of her throat as she pulled my balls into her mouth, sucking. I was gone, gripping her hair, holding her head there as I rode out my orgasm.

A lifetime of this? Yes, please.

CHAPTER 20

ERIN

"Isn't it bad luck to see the bride before the ceremony?" Viktor teased, brushing kisses along my shoulder before fastening the clasp of the diamond necklace on loan from the collection of the royal family's jewels.

"I think we chucked long-standing traditions out the window a while ago." I leaned against him, careful not to disrupt my hair, which was curled, piled and pinned on top of my head, smiling at my reflection in the mirror and the memories of last night that the champagne color of my wedding gown stirred up.

Not just for me, but from the smoldering eyes staring back at me through the reflective glass, Viktor as well.

Butterflies took flight in my stomach, a flurry of excitement and nervous energy like a thousand wings beating inside me. I'd been waiting for this moment with a special surprise for my men, since Henryk opened his arms and his heart to us, claiming us and his life as his own.

Our wedding started in less than an hour, but this was the only ceremony that mattered.

It was just the four of us, alone in our suite, enjoying the last few minutes of peace before the public display was scheduled to begin.

The royal affair was for the world as much, if not more, than it was for us. Reporters have been camping out along the route from the castle to the chapel for the last two days. Liechtenstein's citizens had been camped out even longer. Merchants lined the streets, selling programs filled with pictures, biographies and a complete itinerary of the day's events. There were food vendors selling a wide variety of sweets and savories. The whole thing felt more like a circus than a wedding, but our new celebrity status was something we'd all have to get used to. Thankfully, Henryk had a lifetime of experience navigating these waters.

But all of that could wait. Sharing this private moment with them was more important than anything else happening today. Well, except maybe the start of our honeymoon. Thoughts of stripping them out of their tuxedos brought a blush to my cheeks, leaving me warm, flushed and full of anticipation for the night to come.

"I have something for each of you." The detachable tulle train swished behind me as I crossed the room to retrieve the white gift bag on the high wooden table behind the couch.

Reaching into the shiny paper bag, I pulled out the tissue paper and set three ring boxes on the table, followed by a clear plastic floral container with petite white daisies inside. Each one fastened into a ring using the stems and carefully wrapped floral wire.

Their shared smiles brought tears to my eyes, threatening to ruin the work of the makeup artist who'd left moments before they snuck back into our suite. My heart was full to bursting. Henryk, Viktor and Silas were three quarters of my soul, completing me in a way I'd never known in my adult life.

Yet somehow, I'd known all those years ago when we played together at that playground.

"Erin." Viktor cleared his throat, the emotions overcoming him evident on his face and by the strangled sound of his voice. "This is perfect. Do you have any idea how much we love you?"

"I think I have an inclination." The plastic container opened with a crinkle and crack, the lid popping back, granting access to the delicate rings inside. "I wanted to recreate that moment, something sacred just for us to express our love to one another without the world watching. A memory made just for us, that only we share."

To remove the hint of tarnish Henryk's brother had placed on the original when he shared that story from our childhood without our consent. Bitterness threatened to rise up, but I quelled it down. There was no room for that today or in our future. Every action had a reaction, and without Nicky's actions there was no telling how things would have turned out. He'd tried to tear us apart, to ruin our lives. Instead, he drew us together, fortifying the bond and love we shared.

For that I was grateful... just not enough to invite him to the wedding. His absence was the only scandal any of us would permit. Let the paparazzi have their fun with the black sheep. The most he can be is a distraction every now and then, while we lived our lives in and out of the camera's lens.

"Gentlemen, we're gathered here today to join ourselves in matrimony. A lifetime of wedded bliss."

The crystals embedded into the bodice of my gown and affixed to the nude sheer fabric stretched over my shoulders and across my chest caught the light, sending a shimmer of reflections dancing over their black tuxedo jackets.

"I was going to wait until tonight, but..." Silas slipped his hand into his pocket and pulled out a crumpled sheet of paper. He unfolded the looseleaf sheet, smoothing out the creases against his chest. He cleared his throat and glancing down, proceeded to read the most beautiful, heartfelt vows I had ever heard.

"Erin, Viktor, Henryk, you stole my heart all those years ago when we were little kids. Each of you took an equal share and you never gave it back. It belongs to you. It has all this time." His gaze flicked down to the paper and back to us. "I promise to make you laugh, to surprise you, to fill your days with wonder. To never lie to you. When you stumble, I will be there, arms outstretched, ready to catch you before the fall. To support you in your dreams, to celebrate your wins and share the weight of your losses. To hold your hand as we wind down this path together, never walking in front of you but at your side. I will love you without question or expectation every day for the rest of my life."

Tears streamed down my face, threatening to destroy my makeup and leave me red and puffy before the public ceremony. My chest and throat were tight, emotion making it nearly impossible to speak. My hands shook as I slipped the delicate daisy ring on his finger.

"Dude." Viktor pulled him into a hug, crushing him against his chest and burying his face between Silas's shoulder and his neck, momentarily blocking Henryk and me from the rawness of his emotions.

Viktor wasn't hiding from us, but his defenses, much like his experiences growing up, were different from ours. Silas had been the one constant in his life until serendipity brought Henryk and me back to him. Silas's vows left Viktor vulnerable and in need of the safety and security of the one place he was always able to find that—with Silas. Henryk and I loved him enough not to push, but to give them this moment. I was just grateful to be a part of it. To see how much they meant to each other, how much love they had to give.

I really am a lucky woman.

"Way to raise the bar, bro." Viktor chuckled, sniffling away the tears shimmering in his eyes as he pulled out of their embrace, clapping him on the back one more time before starting his own vows.

"Today in a cathedral, its pews packed with people, and thousands more streaming around the world, I will say I do. But right here, right now, I say I will. I will laugh with you, I will cry with you. I will scream with you when it all feels like it's too much. I will be there for you, day or night. Give me your hand and I will give you forever."

There was a slight tremble in his fingers when I slid the daisy ring over his knuckle. He grasped my hand, holding on as if he were afraid that moment would slip away, and raised it to his mouth, pressing a gentle kiss against my palm.

"Saving the best for last, are we, gentlemen?" Henryk teased, but there was a flicker of uncertainty behind his eyes. He closed his eyes for a moment, as if to center himself, took a deep breath, and let the words pour out of him.

"Truthfully, I'm not sure how to follow that. Despite spending my life preparing for moments like this, I feel woefully unprepared. It's a little frightening and yet exhilarating. Which could also be said for my love for all of you. The three of you have crashed through all my barriers, torn down every wall I built up, destroyed all of my defenses, and have entrenched yourselves in my heart and my soul. You are the water that quenches my thirst, the air that fills my lungs. I am hopelessly and utterly in love with you, and I promise to spend every day of my life proving that to you."

Viktor asked if he could do the honors, then taking the daisy ring from me, placed it on Henryk's finger. It solidified their place in our relationship at each other's side. My heart swelled a little more, pushing against the confines of my ribcage and the boning of my dress.

The words I'd prepared seem inadequate compared to the vows they've made to me and to each other. I decided to chuck the vows I'd memorized in preparation for this moment and speak from my heart.

"Do you remember the day we met?" I paused a moment, smiling at each of them and relishing the sentiment I saw in their eyes. A playful look that said, how could we possibly forget? "I knew when I first saw you—each of you—that we would be together. Forever. The daisies signified the promise that we made to each other all those years ago. I promised my future. My heart. My soul. Today I fulfill that promise and make several more. I promise to give you the best of myself and not shy away from you when I am at my worst. To support you in all things and give my support in return. I give you all of myself, the good, the bad, and the promise of what's yet to come. I give you my love and my heart."

Henryk, Viktor and Silas took turns inching the daisy ring over my finger until it was properly seated, each one stopping to kiss me with a passion that singed my synapses and left me breathless before stepping aside for the next in line.

Promises made, love expressed, we were officially married in the only way that mattered to any of us.

There was a light rap on the door, and Jaque popped his head into the doorway. "It's time. May I?" He motioned to the whole of the suite, asking permission to interrupt. "I want one last chance to check your gown and then we will go. After we arrive, I will make sure the flower girls know how to properly smooth out your train without ripping the lace or detaching it from your waist."

"Are you ready?" Henryk beamed at me, turning that thousand-watt smile on Viktor and Silas.

"Let's get this show on the road." I gave each of them a kiss and shooed them out of the suite, letting Jacque fuss with my gown while we waited for the chauffeur to collect us for the drive to the drive to the cathedral where I will marry my men... for the third time.

Definitely the charm.

CHAPTER 21

HENRYK

My coronation day. My father stepped aside, allowing me to ascend the throne and usher in a new future for our country, for our people. It was almost as surreal as my wedding day. Not the formal ceremony in the cathedral, but the private one shared between Erin, Viktor, Silas and me in our secluded spot within the castle walls.

I turned the platinum ring on my finger, unable to feel the daisies etched along the inside against my skin, but taking comfort in the knowledge that they were there. Erin, our clever beauty, had made arrangements with the jeweler beforehand, ensuring our signature flower, as she called it, withstood the test of time. Unlike the real flowers we wore when we'd spoken our vows to each other. Personal vows, spoken from the heart.

The choir sang the last verse of our anthem. The crowd invited to witness my coronation remained on their feet until the archbishop instructed them to take their seats and proceeded with the same ceremony that has taken place in this cathedral for the reigning monarchs of Liechtenstein for centuries. A modest jewel-encrusted crown rested on a plush red velvet pillow beside a scepter humbly adorned with the same precious stones to create a matching set.

Just like Erin, Viktor, Silas and me.

I watched them from my perch on the throne as they watched me, the adoration flowing both ways. They took my breath away, ratcheting the steady thumping of my heart into an erratic rhythm that left me dizzy and grateful to be sitting down. Collapsing in the midst of the ceremony would make a lasting impression, but not for a strong start of my reign as king of Liechtenstein.

Viktor and Silas were stunning in their white military-cut suits, identical to my own but for the medals and ribbons adorning my chest. Some honorary, some earned. All from military service, a requirement for any king. Or queen, I thought, giving a moment's consideration to the possibility of a daughter and whether I would change the archaic rule or allow her the choice to serve if that was her wish.

Something to discuss with the queen of my heart.

She was glorious, a dainty tiara nestled into the golden crown of curls pinned atop her head. Her white gown reminded me of the dress Cinderella wore when she married her Prince Charming at the end of the animated movie. The long red cape pinned to her shoulders gave her a regal heir befitting a member of the royal court. And yet, as beautiful as she was, looking every bit a queen, nothing compared to the moment I first saw her in her wedding gown. The form-fitting champagne lace contoured her every curve, highlighting the length of her legs and the swell of her breasts while maintaining a modesty appropriate for a royal wedding. The long, detachable train accentuated her narrow waist that I could almost feel beneath my hands.

She was divine, goddess incarnate, and I had forever to worship her. Something I plan to start immediately after the lengthy but necessary ceremony. With the help of Viktor and Silas, of course.

Together in all things, like our love, my success as king of Liechtenstein was entwined with Erin, Viktor and Silas. I needed their support and their unique insights into the decisions I would face as a leader of my country, my people. But most of all, I would need the safety and security only they can provide in our most private moments when I can leave my heart exposed and bare my soul. In the moments when I can lose myself and be the man that I wanted to be—no, the man that I am—and not the man the world needs to see.

Viktor and Silas have transitioned into their roles as advisors and goodwill ambassadors nicely. Their perspective of the investments of developing nations, not just from an infrastructure standpoint but from that of the disenfranchised youth, has been priceless. Viktor's life experiences have given him wisdom and an education not found among my other staff or the high-priced universities they attended, making him uniquely qualified and an immeasurable asset to my cabinet. His pauper-to-prince consort status has made him a media darling and given him the world's ear. When he spoke on issues important to him, people listened. And wrote checks. The same could be said of Silas, whose compassion had helped fill the coffers on a lengthy list of charities. They were making a lasting impact already in the short time since they'd stepped into their roles.

Erin wanted to put her marketing skill to good use, working with Harlowe. I was hesitant at first, worried that the ruthless press would batter her like a hurricane of negativity and eventually wear her down, but our queen was a lioness, too strong and too smart to become a mark for the paparazzi. She continued to assure me that once she felt certain the smudges on my character and negative opinions lingering among the traditionalists that still remained were gone, she would step into a new role. Once she decided which campaigns and causes she'd like to undertake. She had free reign to choose, because whatever it was, she would be brilliant at it.

Like she was with everything.

The archbishop lifted the crown off the pillow with both hands, raising it up as he recited the blessing. Heavy was the head that wore the crown... or so they said. I steeled my spine, my heart and my soul in preparation of the weight about to settle onto my shoulders. Except it didn't. There wasn't the crush of burdening power, crushing my skull and vertebrae, that I had feared and resolved myself to for most of my life. Instead, the crown sat lightly upon my head, just the physical weight of the gold and jewels embedded in it.

Because this responsibility wasn't mine alone. Not anymore.

The rest of the day was a blur. The flash of cameras, cheers of the crowds lining the streets, the procession, and appearance from the castle's main balcony. I'd been looking forward to shedding the formality and relaxing in our apartment within the castle all day. Of course, there were pressing matters that needed my attention. There always would be, but they could wait until the morning. Between the wedding and the coronation, we were on a short timeline. Two life-altering events scheduled almost back-to-back, with crowning me king overlapping our honeymoon. I'd been allotted three weeks and it was nearing the end.

I intend to make the most of it.

The king of Liechtenstein was not just a figurehead. He ruled his country, from the throne and the parliament. I would be expected to do the same. There would be days and nights where I worked long hours, where my attention was divided, and not the least bit equally. It was taxing, demanding and would take its toll, not just on me, but on my family as well. I wanted to spend the last nights of our honeymoon showing them exactly how much I loved and needed them.

Starting now.

"My feet are killing me." Erin tossed the key card to our apartment in the crystal bowl on the buffet table and her purse beside it. "I'm thinking floor-length gowns for these events, like sweeping the floor when I walk, to hide my matching Pumas. I really don't know how Posy does it. Maybe I can get the name of her podiatrist. Because standing in heels for twelve hours? She has to have one on speed dial."

She pressed the tip of one shoe against the heel of the other, ready to toe them off, but I was already on my knees. Slipping one off then then the other, I tossed them by the door and then scooped her up in my arms, heading for the couch.

"Foot massage?" I asked, taking one of her feet in my hands and rubbing my thumbs along the fascia tendon, increasing the pressure slightly with each delicious moan out of her mouth.

Viktor's empty glass hit the highly polished wooden bar top with a thunk, the ice rattling against the crystal with a tink, drawing my attention to the small bar nestled into the corner of the living room. I shared a knowing glance with him and Silas, the three of us in agreement.

We wanted her to moan like that for very different reasons.

Viktor and Silas stalked across the living room like two predators zeroing in on their prey, while my hands worked their way under her skirt and up Erin's silky-smooth legs until my fingertips grazed the edge of her lace panties. Her head fell back against the arm of the couch, and she angled her hips, inching closer until my hand was cupping her. I wasn't the only one who'd been thinking about this all day, because she was already warm, wet and wanting.

And Viktor, Silas and I were more than happy to give her our queen exactly what she wanted. I might be the king of Liechtenstein, but in this domain, Erin ruled. We were hers to command, filling her every need. There was nothing sexier than when she told us exactly how she wanted us to pleasure her.

We took our time undressing, the anticipation and tension rising, heightening the experience until my hands were shaking. A fine sheen of sweat was already forming on my body, and I was on the brink of ravaging her.

I dropped to my knees in front of her, pressing my hand against her thigh until she widened her legs enough for me to bury my face between them, my tongue sliding between her slick folds, dancing over her clit. Her knees buckled, and I tightened my grip on her ass while Viktor and Silas helped support her. Viktor was bent over behind me, one of her breasts in his mouth, while Silas raked his fingers through her hair, lightly fisting her golden mane at the base of her neck just tight enough to elicit a raspy moan from Erin as she watched him stroke himself.

Erin cried out, her body trembling as the first orgasm ripped through her. The first of many. It had been a long day, but it was going to be an even longer night.

I transitioned to my back, pulling Erin down with me. "Tell us what you want."

She positioned us where she wanted us. Me beneath her, Viktor on his knees in front of her, and Silas behind. She slid her slick core along my throbbing dick, rocking her hips until I was fully sheathed inside her and sighed. "Long live the king."

EPILOGUE

ERIN

Six years later

"Henryk, we're going to be late. The plane leaves in ninety minutes." Hurrying around the bathroom, I swiped the bottles of cleanser, toner and moisturizer from the marble countertop and tossed them in my toiletry bag,

"Darling, one of the perks of being royalty is having a plane at our disposal." Henryk picked up the bottle of my favorite perfume and dropped it into the bag, his shoulders shaking with his quiet laughter. "The pilot will wait for us. I promise you."

"I'm not sure I'll ever get used to that. But that's not the point. It's rude to be late, and pretentious to think no one cares if we are, simply because we're royals." I scurried out of the bathroom and tossed my toiletry bag into the suitcase and rummaged through the jewelry box on the counter. "Have you seen my watch?"

"The one on your wrist?" Henryk wrapped me up in his arms, rubbing my back in a lazy, circular motion. "Take a deep breath. That's it. Blow it out slowly. Good. I know the trip has you feeling anxious, but we've planned everything to the most minute detail, and Ray has assembled the best men and women for our security detail.

Harlowe is already in the States waiting for us to arrive. We will be perfectly safe."

"It's not us I'm concerned about." I took another deep breath and exhaled until my lungs felt completely deflated.

"The children are included in the we that I was referring to." Henryk pinched my chin between his thumb and forefinger, tipping and angling my head, and pressed a tender kiss to my lips. "We are going to have a wonderful time celebrating the children's birthday with the rest of our family and friends."

"Of course, I'm excited to see everyone. It's been too long since I visited home." And I was. It had been several months since I had the opportunity to visit my loved ones back home. Motherhood and my work with my charitable foundations didn't afford me the opportunity to travel home nearly as often as I liked. "It's just, this is our first trip out of the country with Gregory and Olivia. I can't help it. I worry."

"Which is why you are such an amazing mother. The children are at the forefront in everything you do." His hands slid around my waist and rested on my swollen belly. "In a couple of months, traveling back to the States won't be an option. At least not until after the baby. Even if the doctor approved, Viktor would be a nervous wreck and eventually wear you down."

"I know." I laughed at Henryk's casual kidding-not-kidding comment. Despite having been through two pregnancies and deliveries, Viktor developed a hovering tendency. More because of his demanding work and travel schedule than anything to do with concerns over a difficult pregnancy. He didn't want to miss anything when he was away and tended to overcompensate when he returned. I was happy to indulge all my doting husbands and expectant fathers when it came to pampering me for nine months.

Foot rubs on demand, with no strings attached? A girl could get used to that.

Everything fell into place shortly after Henryk's coronation. I'd spent the first few months of wedded bliss to three amazing men adjusting to life in and out of the royal spotlight while utilizing my marketing skills to help Harlowe with a rebrand of the monarchy and the subsequent public relations campaign that followed. We had a lot of work to do polishing the tarnish Nicky's grubby fingerprints left on the crown.

The first step was removing him from all active royal duties and annexing him to one of the remotest properties in the king and queen's substantial real estate portfolio. He was given a healthy allowance with even healthier restrictions on how that allowance could be spent. Starting with counseling services. Nicky had plenty of issues to unpack with his therapist and remained out of the spotlight and our hair.

All was forgiven, if not forgotten.

As Viktor and Silas would say, some bridges took longer to mend. They would know, given their original line of work and Viktor's childhood. I had faith that in time, the royal family would be a functional family.

Shortly before our first anniversary, I found my purpose and passion outside our marriage. In truth, I didn't have to look all that hard to find it. Child development. I'd always wanted a family of my own, a house filled with love, laughter and the sounds of rambunctious children running underfoot. Those dreams consisted of a sprawling ranch with a big backyard. Lots of extended family around to support them and be a part of their upbringing. Barbeques in the summer, birthday parties and holidays in good company and good food.

A castle and a royal family were an interesting twist, but provided the perfect platform to ensure children around the world experienced that kind of love and stability. That education and healthcare was not only affordable but attainable. I gave speeches, visited hospitals, raised money for scholarships, tutoring programs, shining a light on the needs of the foster and child welfare systems, doing everything within my power to help. I'd never felt so fulfilled.

Until George was born.

When the queen first presented us with the terms for our marriage, ensuring that the first children born into our new family were Henryk's I worried there would be resentment, or at the very least unwanted tension within our relationship, but my fears were unwarranted. None of that mattered. Except, of course, to the royal line. At four, George was already following in Henryk's footsteps, adored by the paparazzi as the little prince. He looked so much like his father, an adorable miniature version of our king with his dark hair and dark brown eyes, but he was just as much Viktor and Silas's son, a tool belt strapped around his waist whenever they were building something. Like the hope chest for Olivia's room.

With silky gold locks and bright blue eyes, Olivia took after my side of the family. Our little princess has been a joyous addition to our family and had every man in the house wrapped around her pinky finger already, including her big brother.

My heart expanded when Henryk, Viktor, Silas and I were reunited, making room for the three of them to take up permanent residence. I wouldn't have thought it possible to love anyone as much as I did my husbands until our children were born. I immediately wanted more. The large family I always dreamed of wasn't just a dream anymore, it was a reality.

I rubbed my belly, smiling at the life growing inside me. Viktor's first addition to our ever-expanding family. He wanted to be surprised and had spent every spare moment working with Silas to handcraft the furniture for the nursery.

"Mommy!" George and Olivia tumbled into our room, stuffed animals and their favorite blankets in hand for the long flight, excitement beaming in their eyes. "We're going on an airplane today." Olivia copied her brother, the words not quite as clear from our chatty toddler.

"Can I fly the plane?" George asked, fascinated with them ever since Henryk told him of his short stint in the Royal Air Force. The last three birthdays have all been airplane themed. His excitement over his first flight was contagious. "I'm going to be a pilot like you, Daddy." He rushed forward, wrapping himself around Henryk's leg.

"Hmm, how about we start with a tour of the cockpit and work our way up to flying?" Henryk smiled down at George, still clinging to him like a spider monkey, while Henryk lumbered toward the door with the added weight sitting on his foot.

"What about Miss Squish?" I picked up the plush unicorn on the floor by Olivia's feet. "Is she ready to fly?" Her blonde curls bobbing as she nods her head, I scooped her up and settled her onto my hip. "Then we're all set."

"Yes, I believe we are." Henryk beamed at me. The happiness he never thought he deserved because of his royal obligations looked amazing on him.

When I was a little girl, I would pretend that I was a princess waiting for my Prince Charming to whisk me away to his castle where we would live happily ever after. As an adult, it wasn't one of the dreams that I expected to come true. Yet here I am, Queen Consort of Liechtenstein.

And the best part? I have a King and two princes instead of one.

THE END.